Town on Fire

A Twisted Timbers Thriller

Kevin M. Moehring

ISBN: 978-1-7321567-1-5

"He was a giant, when I was just a kid. I was always trying, to do everything he did." -- Zac Brown Band

We all have that person who touched our life in an extraordinary way. That person who treated you as if you were their own child. I was fortunate to have one in my life, a man who made me a better person. My uncle was the best man I ever knew, bringing joy and happiness to the lives of everyone who knew him. He passed away before I turned into the man I am today. I hope I have made him proud. Mikey Joe, this one's for you.

Labor Day Weekend

Thursday

Chapter 1

The old man pulls his black Lincoln into the gravel driveway and up the hill to his modest, but paid-off, house. The home sits on top of a small ridge and like everything else in Twisted Timbers, is surrounded by trees. He worked his whole life to pay off the mortgage, which he was able to accomplish a couple of months back. Now he owns the house outright and there's nothing anyone can do to take it away. His only regret is that his wife Dorothy, who he met in high school, passed away a year before he was able to make the final payment to the bank.

He grabs the bag from the passenger seat of the car and heads into the house. There are several maintenance issues that he notices around the property, but nothing more glaring than the rusted door that his son promised to fix months ago. He hates that he must leave the deadbolt unlocked on the few occasions in which he leaves the house. It isn't a feeling of needing to lock the door, Twisted Timbers is a safe place to live for the most part, but he has spent his whole life accumulating the things inside his home. There are things that evoke memories for him of a lifetime that is now nearing its end.

The wooden stairs that lead to the wrap around porch squeak under the weight of the man. His body was much more formidable in his younger days, but as he reaches his seventieth birthday, he has lost several pounds and his body shows the signs of the times. He enters through the front door and gives a shout to his wife that he's home, even though she's been gone for some time now. Old habits die hard and he refuses to believe that he is living his life alone, something he hasn't done since he got married.

The cancer came quick for Dorothy and her struggle was a short one. When you lose the person that you spent your entire life with, you no longer know how to live alone. His days are filled with reading his favorite crime books, reminiscing over the times he shared with his wife, and arguing with his son, Harry.

He knows the boy is busy but ever since his mother passed away, he hardly ever comes home and refuses to carry on a conversation with his father that doesn't end in him storming out. The old man can only look at the deteriorating relationship with his son from a distance. It is hard enough for the man to get around, chasing his busy son would be virtually impossible.

The old man checks his son's room every morning, and feels the disappointment when he sees the bed has not been slept in. He has no idea where Harry spends his nights, nor does he care. He knows he raised his son better than how he is acting, so the old man could care less what the boy is doing. The death of his mother was hard on Harry, but it was hard on the old man as well. His son has his own job, an important job, and several people in his life to keep him busy. Dorothy passed away shortly after the old man retired from the high school, where he taught for almost as long as they lived in this run-down house. Since she left, he has lived his life virtually alone.

He thinks about getting something to eat from the fridge but the ride home from Portland took more out of him than he thought it would. He places the bag of books on the table next to his easy chair, his favorite place in the house. Usually at this time of evening he would turn the news on the television, with the sound turned down, and read until he fell asleep in the chair. Tonight however, he doesn't feel like watching the news and seeing his son's face, which is plastered on the screen with increasing regularity.

The old man grabs a crocheted blanket from the pile near the couch and has a seat in his chair. This blanket is his favorite that Dorothy ever made, and she made many. This one is softer than the others, maybe due to the fabric or maybe she did a new kind of stitch pattern, either way he loves the way it hugs his aging body. He plops down in the chair and reaches for the bag of books he bought at the booksellers in Portland. His son told him he could just have his books shipped to the house to save the trip into the city, but the old man likes the smell of fresh books and enjoys talking to the women who work at the store. He spent his life studying the English language, and teaching it, and believes some things just don't get better with advances in technology. Being able to look a person in the face while discussing a book is one of the things the old man has loved for many years.

He searches through the paperbacks for the book he wants to start tonight, the latest Stephen King thriller. He is not usually a fan of King, but the nice lady in the store told him this book was more of a mystery and less gory than the works that made the author famous. He opens the book to the dedication page and instantly remembers that it isn't just the gore that turned him away from King books, but also the profanity. He has no issue if the words are integral in the telling of the story, but to go so far as to include them in the dedication is preposterous to the old-timer. He slams the book shut and puts it on the side table and grabs a different paperback from the bag. Before he can even check to see which one he picked up, hoping for the latest Stephanie Plum book, his breath is taken away by two large hands that have grabbed ahold of his neck.

He feels helpless. Whoever has ahold of him is strong and has leverage on him by standing behind the chair. He can feel the muscles in his neck being squeezed, making it impossible to scream for help or even swallow. He can feel the tears forming on the corner of his eyelids as he struggles to open them. Once he does, he is confronted by a stranger standing in front of him. The thought of these men being in his home sends a shiver of fear through his body. This was not what he had in mind when he prayed for companionship in his life.

The person in front of him is much younger than the old man and Hispanic. The caramel skin tone and dark hair gives away his ethnicity right away. His locks are tucked under a Giants ball cap and he stands in front of the old man with just enough of a smile to show the missing tooth on the right side of his mouth. The look in the foreigner's eyes is unlike anything the old man has ever seen before. It is the look of someone who has bad intentions. The look of someone who always has bad intentions.

The old man has no idea who is standing behind him but judging by the strength in his hands it has to be someone powerful. He can almost feel his esophagus crumble under the pressure. No one has said a word in the few seconds since his breath was taken away. He sits there staring at the man in front of him, trying to figure out what they are doing here. He doesn't have much cash in the house, anyone who looked at the dilapidated structure from the outside would surely know that, so he quickly rules out that these guys are here to rob the place.

The intruder in front of him pulls the toothpick from his mouth, which the old man hadn't even noticed, and begins to speak in broken English. "Que pasa? You have money? Our boss wants the money you owe him, or mi hermano will squish your neck like a raisin."

The old man feels the hands on his neck loosen for the first time, allowing air to flow almost normally. He heard the words the man said, which makes his skin crawl at the poor grammar and combination of two different languages flowing together in one thought, but he doesn't know how to respond. What money are they looking for and who is their boss? Did he just call the other guy his brother? That is the translation of hermano as far as the old man knows. He taught English, not Spanish, but faintly remembers hearing the term in something that he read several years ago. Either way, it makes no difference what he called the guy with the strong hands, the old man has no idea who these men are and what they want.

He says nothing. He simply stares back at the man with a puzzled look, focusing more on breathing and staying alive than giving in and telling the man he has no idea what he is talking about. This obviously angers the dark-skinned man as he raises his ball cap, rubs his hand through his already slicked back hair and forcefully throws the hat against the couch. He looks at the old man in disdain and inches closer to the chair.

"Phew, you a tough old gringo, huh? I will show you who's tougher, hombre." He reaches for the plastic bag on the side table and dumps out the remaining books onto the floor. Quickly, the Mexican throws the bag over the old man's head as his brother maneuvers his hands to hold it tight against the man's face. The slow stream of air that his body was getting moments earlier, has now been cut off completely. Every breath is a struggle, the warmness of the air hitting his throat letting him know the oxygen is quickly running out.

Chapter 2

The old man has barely moved, resigned to the fact that these two men are bigger and younger, an advantage he lost decades ago. He tries to control his breathing as best as he can, but when there is no air to breath, controlling it is impossible. His body remains still. He has read enough crime books to know that in situations like this a person is best served by staying calm. Flailing about will only increase your heart rate and cause your body to need more oxygen to survive, more oxygen that his body is currently being deprived of.

He listens intently but hears nothing coming from outside of his plastic cocoon. He runs through his mental rolodex, looking for anyone of Hispanic ethnicity that he may have borrowed money from in the past. He can't think of a single person. There have not been too many foreigners that have come to Twisted Timbers in the last forty years, so it doesn't take long for the man to decide that these men must be looking for someone else. He just hopes he will be given the opportunity to convince them of that before they kill him.

A long period of silence allows the old man to gather his thoughts. When he was teaching, in the later years when the kids felt much more entitled, he practiced a meditation technique that Dorothy taught him. She would have him close his eyes and focus on being alone in a cave. He was only allowed to picture things in his mind that were his favorites, a new book, a well written essay from a student, this soft blanket on his legs. This technique worked at calming him down, especially thinking about the blanket. When the Mexican man got close enough to put the bag over his head, he must have stepped on the bottom of it, causing it to slide down the old man's legs. He reaches down with his brittle hands and pulls it back up over his lap.

That's the moment he realizes it. His hands are not bound and the main thing that is restricting his breathing is a cheap plastic bag. He reaches up and rips the thin bag apart, gasping for the freshness of the air that tickles his senses. He takes three long breaths before he thinks to look around for the guy that was standing in front of him.

He hears the footsteps come from around the corner, from the kitchen, but he can't turn his head to see who it is. His fears are realized when he hears the accent and horrible grammar again.

"Hooray for the old-time fart. He must be a smarty pants. Usually it takes much longer for people to reach for the bag and rip it." He once again looks at the old man with a slimy smile, one that has no sympathy for the pain the man is feeling in his neck. "Now, old man, I am going to ask you some questions and you need to tell the truth."

The old man squirms a little in his chair, feels the blood surging through the hands that grip his neck and looks at the man in front of him. He knows he will tell this man anything he wants to know, as long as it gets them out of his house. He simply nods, refusing to speak and feel the burn in his windpipe that will come along with it.

"El Carnicero wants his money. Do you have his money?" Every final syllable the man speaks is drawn out for a beat or two too long.

Who is El Carnicero and why would I owe him money? The old man has no idea what the man in front

11

of him is talking about and the translation of the name is lost on him. As versed as he is in the English language, he is equally as ignorant when it comes to foreign languages. He shakes his head as much as he can, letting the man in the Giants cap know that he has no money for anyone.

"Wrong answer!" The man with the toothpick in his mouth screams, raises his hand high into the air and before the old man can react, the Mexican slams a butcher knife into his left hand. The tip of the knife goes through the soft fleshy portion of skin just behind the knuckles and completely through the hand, embedding itself in the padding and wooden frame of the arm rest of the chair.

For a moment the thug chuckles out loud, happy that his melee hit its intended target. The old man grabs for the knife with his good arm, but his efforts are only rewarded with tighter squeezing from the faceless man who diligently stands post behind him.

"Ok hombre, let's try this again. This is the Billings house, it says so on the mailbox out front. I know this is the Billings house and the man that owes El Carnicero money is named Billings, Harry Billings.

It does not take a rocket surgeon to see that you must be him." The Hispanic man looks pleased at himself and gives a slight nod to the man behind the chair, who in turn releases most of the pressure from the old man's neck.

"I am Harold Billings, Harry is my son. I have not seen him in a few days."

"Wrong answer again!" shouts the Mexican. With great accuracy he slams a second knife through the right hand of the old man. It went through his skin in exactly the same spot, once again becoming lodged in the wood beneath the cushion of the arm rest.

The senior Billings tries to scream, but his words are muted by raspy breaths. He looks down at the blood that has begun to trickle down his pale skin from the knife wounds. He is pinned to his chair, unable to free himself. He finally gets his first look at the man who had remained hidden up until now, keeping a vice-like grip on his neck and blocking his airway. If the first man called him his brother, then they are the oddest pair of siblings Mr. Billings has ever seen. This second man stands head and shoulders above the first man, with broad shoulders and muscles that seem to be jumping out of his under-sized shirt.

The two visitors turn their back to the old man, without looking at each other. The talker of the two stops before reaching the door and turns back. "We'll be back gramps. Don't go anywhere." The smaller man intended this statement as a joke, but the Mexican men were the only ones laughing, letting out loud whoops as they slammed the front door behind them.

As he sits in his living room, stuck to the chair by the sharp knives from his very own kitchen, the old man can't help but worry about his son. His son has always been mischievous, to say the least, but this time it looks like he may be in a little over his head. The old man vows that he will call Sheriff Thompson as soon as he frees himself, if he doesn't pass out first. He laughs slightly to himself, not at the severity of his current situation but at the Stephen King book that was tossed on the floor and landed with the dedication page facing outward. The same line that turned the old man off on the book now seems ominously relevant. Four words that the old man didn't appreciate in the context of the dedication, but they become more meaningful after the events of the last few minutes. "Shit don't mean shit."

Chapter 3

There has been no need for Sheriff Mitch Thompson to set an alarm clock for the last month and a half. Since they have been together, no matter how late they are up, Sloane Nichols is out the door on her morning run and back in the apartment before he begins to stir in bed. She usually greets him with a kiss as he starts to wipe the sleep from his eyes, but today is his off day. The last off day before the end of the tourist season. In four short days, Twisted Timbers will hold the annual Labor Day Parade marking the final days of the busy season. Soon, the town will resort back to the way it is for eight months of the year, before the temporary shops open and the campgrounds become overcrowded with city folks looking for relaxation.

Sloane has let him sleep in this morning, but he watches her move around the kitchen. Like she normally does, she has found one of his old shirts to put on after showering. He loves the way her body looks in it. The shirt covers just enough of her body to leave Mitch wanting to see the rest. She shuffles about, making coffee and a bagel in his kitchen, with no clue that he has been checking her out for the last five minutes.

He doesn't remember when it was assumed that she would start living with him, but he's not upset about it. It's nice having someone else in the apartment, especially someone who makes his old shirts look that good. Their relationship started out innocently enough, but after only a couple of weeks, they had become more serious and exclusive. She now must know that he is watching her because she does a sexy spin in her bare feet and raises the bottom of the shirt slightly. He loves her legs, even though he has no desire to join her in the hours of running she does to keep them that way.

He knows he's been caught looking at her when she heads for the bedroom with two mugs. He follows her with his eyes as she sets the mugs on the nightstand, still refusing to acknowledge that she knows he's awake. Like she had been shot from a cannon she hurls herself across the bed and lands on top of Mitch, her muscular legs straddling his body.

"I caught you, you perv!" The smile stretches across her face and her still damp hair falls to the left side of her face. "You know, you could get into a lot of trouble for looking at girls that way."

"The way I see it Miss, this is my apartment. If women don't want me to look at them that way, they shouldn't stand half naked in my kitchen." He has gotten used to her odd sense of humor a little quicker than he thought he would. She was raised by men, so it was peculiar at first that she would find the same things funny that Mitch did.

The last six weeks have flown by in his mind. It seems like it was just yesterday when he had wondered if he had a chance with the older woman. Not only did he have a chance with her, but she made the first move, much to his delight. She came on strong, like how she is perched on top of him at the moment. He loves the smell of her body and the way her skin feels when it touches his.

"There are men in this world who would pay good money to have half-naked women bring them coffee in the morning. You should consider yourself lucky." She ends this sentence with a light kiss on his neck.

"Lucky? Is that what I should feel?" He grabs her waist and spins her over in a quick flip. It is effortless to spin himself on top of her and he leans in for a kiss. As his lips gets closer to hers, and she begins to return the gesture, he pulls back, teasing her even more. "If I was really lucky, you would have brought me bacon and eggs along with the coffee."

She shoves him off from on top of her in a playful manner and gives him a couple of soft jabs to his ribs. "Isn't that what Maddie's Diner is for?"

"It's my first off day in a couple of weeks, I was hoping to not leave the apartment today." The thought of vegging around the apartment sounds even better when he says it out loud than it did in his head when he thought about it every day for the last week. He pulls Sloane back on top of him, in the position he prefers. He can feel the excitement building in his body as she moves her hips slightly. She collapses on top of his chest and allows her lips to touch his. The embrace is intense, as they all have been since the first one.

They have done this enough that Mitch knows where her sensitive spots are. He knows just where to touch her to bring out the soft moans that turn him on.

Unfortunately, he isn't able to tease these areas for too long as they are distracted by the ringing of his cell phone. They ignore the first series of rings but when the caller persists, and the happy little beeps of the ringtone fail to go away, they both know playtime is on hold. She gives him a look that lets him know she understands that he has to answer the phone, being the sheriff of a town definitely has its drawbacks.

She reluctantly climbs off of him but allows her hand to trace around the bulge that is showing in his boxers. He grabs the phone, recognizes the number and answers it in a huff. "Hey Stuart. What can I do for ya?"

"Sheriff, I'm sorry to be calling, I know it's your off day, but I think you might want to turn on the news. I'm down here working the press conference about that new resort development, and I'm almost certain I see a familiar face."

Mitch can hear the panic in his most trusted deputy's voice. Mitch reaches for the remote control, which stays on Sloane's side of the bed since she moved in. He clicks the power button and turns through the channels until he finds the local news. The camera is showing a press conference outside the vacant lot on the south side of town. Mitch recognizes the part of town along with a few of the faces on the stage. Mayor Billings is currently at the microphone but with the volume down Mitch can only look at the man. Behind him is a stunning female, who he assumes is Cassie Reynolds, the CEO of the Reynolds Corporation, the company that is behind the proposed development.

"Stuart, I have the news on. I'm not sure what I'm supposed to be looking at, but whatever it is, I'm not seeing it." Mitch has to hold the phone away from his mouth to tell Sloane to stop what she is doing. She has worked her hand under the elastic at the top of his shorts and is using her nails to tickle his skin.

"Look next to Ms. Reynolds, slightly behind her. I know it's him." Stuart stops talking and allows the sheriff enough time to scan the rest of the faces on the stage.

Mitch scoots down to the foot of the bed, trying to see who Stuart is trying to point out. Directly behind the woman with the expensive looking jewelry, standing firm and at attention, is a face Mitch recognizes. At first, he thought he must have been mistaken, but this man's face has been embedded in his mind since the night at Graham Park.

"Stuart, I see him. I can't believe it, but that's him. That's Jesse Meyers!"

Chapter 4

Mitch hangs up the phone and tosses it on the nightstand. He looks at Sloane, who had been playfully kissing his bare back while he was talking to Stuart. He knows she is expecting a session of love making, but right now, that is the furthest thing from his mind. All he can think about is the man he saw on the television. That sure did look like Jesse Meyers, but he would have to have some nerve to return to town after how he left, Mitch thinks to himself.

He softly nudges Sloane off him and turns in the bed to face her. She already has the defeated look of a kid who has had their favorite toy taken away from them unexpectedly. Mitch had wanted to spend the day together as badly as she did, but circumstances have changed. He can't ignore what he saw, nor can he let Jesse think that he can come and go as he pleases. He also has a beautiful woman sitting in his bed, wanting a chance to be intimate.

He doesn't even get a chance to open his mouth and speak before Sloane tells him that she understands. She is a good woman, in fact she is a great woman.

They have not had much time over the past few weeks to explore their relationship. Most of the time they have spent together, they had been too busy exploring each other's bodies to worry about where the relationship was going. He has been holding on to the fact that the end of the tourist season is only a few days away, and once things calm down in town, they will have much more time together.

Reluctantly, Mitch stands up and walks away from the bedroom. He has intentions of taking a quick shower and making his way to the press conference and confronting the former soldier before he can slip away again but leaving Sloane alone in the bedroom was the last thing he wanted to do on his off day. He gives her a last glance before heading into the bathroom. She doesn't see him looking at her as she rubs lotion on her legs. He loves her scent. He loves her body. He loves everything about this woman, but he hates that he has disappointed her.

After a quick shower, Mitch stands in front of the steamy mirror and looks at himself. At the beginning of the year he was the youngest member of the police force, fighting desperately to prove himself to the others, especially his father. A few short months later and he is the man in charge. His eyes show the signs of sleep deprivation and stress that comes along with the job. He rubs the towel over his long brown locks and hangs it back on the rack, something he never did before Sloane moved in.

Lots of things in his life have changed since they began dating, none bigger than his ability to once again enjoy life. His father stressed so much the importance of the job that he caused his son to dread going to work every day. The force as it stands today, the three members, all enjoy the company of one another, making the long hours more bearable. Sloane has allowed Mitch to be himself, never bringing the office into the bedroom. He loves the way she makes him feel, much different than he can remember feeling before. When they are in the office, Sloane is just as much one of the guys as any male officer would be, an attribute Mitch finds appealing. She is just as sexy to him when she comes back from a run and is covered in sweat, as she is when she spends hours getting ready and putting on her makeup.

There is rarely a day that goes by when he doesn't find himself doing strange or funny things that he would have never thought to do before she came into his life, like putting the toilet seat back down or not drying his hands with the fancy towels that are only for guests. He is thankful for her more than she realizes. He looks at his image again in the mirror and vows that he will make this up to her. He owes it to her. Once the season is over and things in Twisted Timbers calm down during the winter, he will make it all up to her.

Right now, though, he needs to get dressed and head into town, but not before he gives Sloane a little show and excitement. She is usually the one who is making him forget about work by doing silly things, usually leading to sex. He wants to show her that he can let loose as much as she can. He turns and grabs the towel from the rack and gathers it on both ends. He straddles the towel, still completely naked, and looks again at himself in the mirror. Six months ago, he would never think about doing something like this, but this girl, this woman, has a way of making him do just about anything, and he kind of likes it.

With his trusty cowboy hat on his head, and damp towel between his legs, Mitch leaps out of the bathroom and begins to trot around the room as if the towel is his horse. He gallops around the bed several times singing at the tops of his lungs, "I'm a cowboy, baby! I'm a cowboy, baby!"

He doesn't really know the song too well, he's only heard it a few times when Sloane would have it on while she made dinner. His act has achieved the goal, she is rolling around in the bed, laughing hysterically. One final lap around the bed and he tosses the towel high into the air and climbs on top of her. She wraps her legs around his and he leans into her. He looks her right in the eyes, her comically tearful eyes, and lets the stare linger for a moment.

"I'm sorry I have to leave. I would love to stay in bed with you all day." He can feel her breath on his skin, his body still warm from the shower. "I promise when things slow down, I will make it up to you.

"When you make it up to me, will you do this dance again?" She uses the strength of her lower body to roll him over and climb on top of him. Sloane takes the hat from his head and swings it around, bucking her hips at the same time. "Now I'm a cowboy, baby!" she cries out, mimicking his naked dance.

"This was a one-time performance. In the future, I'll dance around to a song I know all the words to, unfortunately for you, the list of songs is limited to Happy Birthday and The Star-Spangled Banner." He allows her to remain on top of him for a few more seconds, breathing in the smell of her lotion.

"Well that should be a rather unique performance, but if I come home and find you hanging from the ceiling fan clucking like a chicken, I'm leaving you." She gives him a long, deep kiss and climbs off his lap and reaches for the remote control.

"Hey! Have you been spying on me again? How do you know what I do when you're at work?" He gives her a firm slap on the butt cheek, strong enough to leave a light pink handprint but not so hard that she dislikes it.

Sloane pretends to ignore him as he finishes getting dressed. He refrains from wearing his uniform, he doesn't want this meeting to appear to be official in any capacity. He knows the town leaders are counting on the new development plans from Ms. Reynolds and he doesn't want a confrontation between himself and the man from Graham Park to hamper the negotiations. He dresses casually, clean jeans and a polo shirt. Although he contemplated wearing it, he has decided to leave the cowboy hat laying on the bed.

Mitch walks back into the bedroom where he finds Sloane studiously eying a talk show on the television. She loves to watch the talk shows, especially the ones with the panel of female hosts who love to rip apart the Hollywood gossip. Mitch could care less about what's on the television, but he never leaves her these days without giving her a kiss. They both know how dangerous their jobs can be. She hardly looks up at him when he kisses the top of her head, a sure sign that she is as disappointed in the change of plans as he is. While the naked dance might have eased the tension a bit, it did not take away all the angst over the situation.

"This shouldn't take too long, at least I hope it doesn't. When I get back would you want to go out and get some dinner?" It still feels weird to Mitch that sometimes he must woo a woman that shares his bed. The truth is, everything he knows about relationships, he has learned in the past few weeks. It is his last chance to take Sloane around town to show her some of the places that pop up only during the summer months. They might not be able to spend the day together like they had planned, but he could still show her a good time.

She looks up at him with her blue eyes, and a smile crosses her face. He loves to see her smile, not only because it means that what he said made her happy, but her smile is the sexiest thing about her. He loved it from the very first time he saw it. She stands up from the bed, gives him a tight hug, then slaps his butt and gives him a pal-like "get out of here."

Chapter 5

The streets of Twisted Timbers are predictably quiet. It's Thursday morning and kids are back in school already. By Friday afternoon the town will be overflowing with visitors looking to celebrate one last weekend before the cold and snow of winter hit the area. The now empty parking lots will be full of travel trailers, SUVs and minivans within twenty-four hours, but Mitch is able to navigate down Main Street without much trouble.

The gathering outside the City Council office, which is nothing more than a storefront complete with oversized window, has mostly dissipated. A few remaining cameramen are taking shots of the large cardboard signage that had been placed next to the podium, the same podium Mitch had seen during the newscast earlier in the morning. Two large Chevy Tahoes are still parked in front of the building, both black with very dark tinted windows. Mitch pulls in and parks his truck behind them.

He hurries out of the truck and scans the faces for Stuart Johnson. The deputy is nowhere to be seen.

The only face Mitch recognizes is that of Mayor Billings, complete with wire rimmed glasses and already smoking a celebratory cigar. Mitch decides to avoid the mayor and heads straight for the first of the two Chevys. He taps on the dark passenger side window and makes the motion with his hand for whomever is inside to roll it down.

Several seconds pass and Mitch begins to think that the vehicle may be empty. He begins to walk ahead to the second of the two cars, the one that was parked in front of the empty one. As he nears the passenger side window, the car is put into gear and drives off. Mitch is left standing on the curb watching it head down Main Street and make a left onto Highway 30 and out of sight. He turns again to the vehicle he knocked on earlier, the front windshield is less dark than the side windows and he can see several passengers inside.

As Sheriff Thompson begins to head back to the car, he can see the driver putting the car into gear. He reacts quickly and jumps out into the road, reaching for his badge at the same time. He stands inches from the front bumper of the oversized vehicle, his arm at a right angle, showing the badge for the driver to see. The man behind the wheel pauses momentarily before giving Mitch the sign to come around to the side. Now standing in the middle of the street, Mitch waits for the driver to open the window, and is shocked when the rear window slowly rolls down instead.

He is met by the face of a stunning woman. A woman he has seen on the television and has heard about but has never met. Her skin is pale, her hair is blonde, and her smile is captivating. This is Cassie Reynolds, the millionaire entrepreneur who has come to town in hopes of opening a year-round resort. The mayor has been harping on the fact that she was going to be in town and that Mitch needed to take extra precautions, but judging by the number of security personnel she has around her, there wouldn't be much for the sheriff to do.

"Hello, I'm Sheriff Thompson," he begins.

"I know who you are, Sheriff, what can I do for you?" Her voice comes from the back seat and she refuses to allow her eyes to meet his.

"I'm looking for one of your guards, a Jesse Meyers." He waits patiently for a response from the woman. He hadn't really expected to be meeting her for the first time under these circumstances, but here they are.

"I have no one under my employment by that name. Now if you don't mind, I have places to be. My time is very valuable." She begins rolling the window up and Mitch scrambles to place his hand on it before it reaches the top.

"I saw him standing behind you during the press conference. I know it was him. He's a little over six feet tall, broad in the shoulders, buzzed hair and was a former Army Ranger. Does any of this ring a bell?" Mitch turns his head to look into the front seat. Both bodyguards are looking straight ahead but he can see enough to realize they both fit the description.

"I told you once Sheriff, I know of nobody by that name. Now if you don't mind, you are scaring my son. He doesn't like police officers. They make him nervous." The young boy in the bench seat next to the woman has not moved in the few seconds since the window came down, his attention drawn completely by the electronic gaming unit he holds.

Mitch takes a step back, more into the middle of the street. The window raises, and the dark car drives away down Main Street. Mitch is left standing in the middle of the road, wondering if his eyes played tricks on him and it really wasn't Jesse Meyers that he saw on the television. Maybe Stuart was also suffering from the same poor eyesight, or maybe the infamous Jesse Meyers has changed his identity. It wouldn't be too hard for a man with his background to get a new name and continue living a normal life, putting his past far behind him.

A car horn rattles his mind back to the present and Mitch quickly jumps back to the sidewalk. He hears someone yell profanities from the car that passes, a shiny new silver Lexus, and he catches enough sight of the driver to realize that it was Mayor Billings, who was obviously in some sort of hurry. To say that Mitch is a fan of the mayor would be a lie. He detests the man. His cheap suits, the aroma of cigar that surrounds him and his slicked back hair all make him look like the stereotypical scumbag politician, a stereotype that Mitch believes describes the mayor perfectly. The man is constantly on the sheriff's back about keeping things in order, telling Mitch where the department should focus their efforts on the crowded weekends. Dealing with the mayor is a necessary evil. At least it is if Mitch wants to keep his job.

Finally, Mitch spots Stuart Johnson. The senior deputy has just come out of one of the trendy Seattle-based coffee shops that show up during the summer months and disappear when the temperatures drop, and coffee is really needed. He watches as Stuart licks the whipped cream off the top of his drink, a murky liquid that resembles muddy water more than it does coffee. Mitch checks the traffic and makes the sprint across the street to catch up with the deputy, who appears to be enjoying his drink.

"Hi Sheriff. Sorry to drag you out on your off day. I hope it didn't cause too many issues at home." Stuart leans against the side of the brick building which holds the post office, a bank and the licensing bureau.

"All in a day's work. I have no idea how you can drink that crap. I'd rather drink out of the toilet." He turns his nose up as he points to the cup in Stuart's right hand.

"Aw, it's not so bad. It's expensive though. I guess all the sugar they put in here is what gets people addicted to the stuff. Did you catch up with our man?"

Stuart takes a long drink and eyes the sheriff from over the cup.

"Unfortunately, I was too late. I did however get to speak to the ever-pleasant Cassie Reynolds. She swore to me that none of her employees go by that name."

"Sheriff, that's impossible. I know what I saw, and it was him," Stuart rebukes.

"I think so too. All it means is our former Ranger changed his identity in the five months since Graham Park. I doubt it would be too hard for a guy with his background." Mitch says this in a manner that sounds like he is trying to convince himself as much as he is Stuart.

"I guess you're right. Are you going to try to arrest him? I mean if he is not doing anything wrong or killing anyone, I don't see any harm. If he has assumed a new identity, it may be hard for us to prove he is not who he says he is." Stuart tilts the cup high above his head in order to get the last drops of the drink into his mouth. He licks his lips in approval once he is happy that he has gotten all the sugary satisfaction he could from the cup.

"I hadn't really thought about that Stu. I would still like to have a conversation with the man. I'm sure I will have my chance, I don't see Ms. Reynolds leaving town anytime soon." He had watched the newscast long enough to read the scrolling information that stated the Reynolds Corporation had intended to break ground in less than a month.

"I'm sure he'll be around. What are your plans for the rest of the day? You're more than welcome to join me as I walk around the town." Stuart looks at him with wide eyes, the caffeine already doing its job.

"No thanks. I have a woman at home who is somewhat unhappy with me. I promised to spend the day with her since we were both off, we haven't had much time together lately." The relationship with Sloane has not necessarily been the best kept secret in town, but this is the first time that Mitch has talked openly about it to anyone. He was enjoying the time he spent with Sloane so much, that he didn't want to jeopardize it by talking about it. More importantly, he didn't like the image it portrayed that the sheriff was sleeping with one of his deputies.

"This weekend is sure to be a busy one. You two should enjoy the day. I'll see you in the office in the morning." Stuart tosses the cup into the green trash can on the corner and starts strolling down Main Street, waving to almost every pedestrian and store owner as he passes by. Stuart is a good egg, and a man Mitch is happy to have on his side. A true believer that Twisted Timbers is the best place to call home.

Chapter 6

The old man is lost in a dream. A dream about the only woman he ever loved. She is skipping down the trail, the one that she used to walk on almost every day. The sun shines through her hair, creating a halo of light around her head. He can't make out her features, but when you have spent the majority of your life with the same woman, you tend to notice the little things that make her unique. The way they walk. The way they smell. The way they tilt their head to the side when they are trying to understand something you are explaining to them, like early nineteenth century prose.

He has forgotten about his current situation. The pain in his hands has gone away completely, mostly because they are now numb. It's been several hours since the two Hispanic men entered his home and viciously pinned him to the chair. He thought surely his son would call, which he tries to do almost every day. The old man had hoped Harry would become worried when there was no answer and make his way over to see if everything is alright. As he looks out at the midday sun shining through the trees in front of his living room window, he has not heard a single ring from the phone mounted on the wall in the hallway.

He closes his eyes again, trying anything he can to keep his attention off the two butcher knives protruding from his hands. When it first happened, it felt like he could feel the blade slice through every muscle. Now there is no feeling at all. He tries to return his focus to the memories of Dorothy, his sweet Dorothy. Just as her face is beginning to form in his mind, he is snapped out of the haze by the sound of a vehicle coming up the gravel driveway. The driveway snakes around the house so he can't see who it is. He sits quietly waiting for whoever it is to knock or come through the front door. He waits several seconds and then the eagerness is more than he can bear. He begins screaming as loudly as he can, hoping that whoever it is will hear his pleas for help and he can finally get these knives out of his flesh. His voice comes out muddled from the dryness of his throat caused by the panicked breaths while his head was inside the bag.

No one comes. His screams fall silent. Was he imagining the sound of the car? Has the pain caused his mind to begin making things up? He doesn't feel like he is going crazy, but he has been around long enough to know that the mind is a feeble thing. He closes his eyes once more and begins to picture the face of his late wife again. He squeezes his lids tight, trying hard to allow the image to come into focus. The more he struggles with his recollection, the more everything in his mind's eye is a blur.

Again, more abruptly this time, he is brought back to the reality of his predicament. He feels pain in his left hand again. Excruciating pain. He opens his eyes and the larger of the two Hispanic men is standing in front of him with the knife that had been stuck in the old man's hand, now raised in the air. The man reaches for the knife in the right hand and yanks it out as well. The old man screams in agony. Quickly, he is silenced by the grunt of a voice that comes from the big man.

"Silence gringo."

The senior Billings whimpers, holding his hands out in front of his body as if he is showing them to the large Mexican. The big man pays no attention and produces a thick rope that he tightly wraps around the prisoner's body, securing him once again to his favorite chair. Confident that he has tied the knot properly, the large man sits silently on the couch opposite the chair, staring at Mr. Billings like a prized fighter would look down on his fallen opponent. The two men engage in a staring contest, one man resembling a lion stalking its prey and the other, the poor gazelle who knows he will soon shed blood.

"You have me mistaken for someone else," the old man pleads.

His faint words provoke no change in the expression of the large man. His scowl sends beams of confidence across the room before he speaks. "I said silence gringo! El Carnicero is on his way to see you."

Chapter 7

With an entire day ahead of him and zero plans, Mitch piles back into his truck and heads to the one place that he has been avoiding for the last four months. The town cemetery is an eerie place, even in the bright sunshine. Mitch Thompson has dreaded coming here to see his father, the finality of death lingering over the tombstones like a dense fog that rolls in off the ocean.

Many of the grave sites are overgrown with tall grass and weeds. In a town of this size, the chore of maintaining a burial site falls on the family of the deceased. Mitch would be embarrassed to tell anyone that he has not visited his father's grave since the burial. He uses his hectic life as an excuse, to fool himself into thinking that he had intentions on coming earlier in the summer but simply got too busy.

As he makes his way down the hill, looking at the markers without really reading the names carved on them, Mitch is suddenly hit with a feeling of nostalgia. He can practically hear his father's booming voice telling him to take out the trash or tidy up his room. It's odd that whenever he looks back on his life growing up, the things he remembers are the things he hated most about his father. The discipline he demanded and the way that anything the old man told him was expected to be obeyed. Is this why Mitch is the man he is today or is it the reason that Mitch has never really been able to cry over the loss of his father?

It's not hard to find his father's grave, it's the largest tombstone in the small cemetery, a fact that was not lost on the city council who graciously took it upon themselves to handle the burial. The large marble obelisk sits in the middle of the grassy area, almost segregated from the rest of the markers. It stands high above the rest like an awkward grade school boy who has hit his growth spurt far before the rest of the class.

Mitch is relieved to see that there is no sign of overgrowth near the headstone. All the grass has been meticulously trimmed and the brambles that are common in areas like this, have failed to grab ahold of the stone structure. Mitch feels a bit of guilt looking at the pristine nature of the column, knowing that someone has taken great care of it. It should be him who is here on a weekly basis, trimming the bushes and cutting the grass, not someone who is not family.

The flowers that were laid on the grave at burial have all wilted together in a pile of brown leaves and off-colored petals. They have been left by whomever has been tasked with keeping the area neat, allowed to retire into the earth or be carried away by the breeze that whips through the valley. Mitch kneels next to the stone, careful to not disturb the remnants of the flowers or any of the other signs of remembrance that have been left.

His father was beloved in this town, the outpouring of remorse from the residents overwhelmed Mitch in the days after the funeral. Looking down at this memorial of his father and the dozen or so trinkets that have been left by visitors over the months, reinforces the feeling of respect his father garnered. Even this long after the funeral, Mitch still hears condolences daily, usually from the old-timers in town that may be forgetful of the fact that they wished him the same sentiment a week or two earlier.

Mitch begins talking to his father, or the spirit of his father. He is not really sure how the whole thing is supposed to work, and he feels a bit silly talking to a piece of marble. He continues talking anyway. Mitch talks about what happened at Graham Park after his father was killed, how he was able to find the men in the cave in the woods before they were able to do any more damage to the visitors and how the entire town is buzzing with excitement over the thought of a year-round resort opening in the future.

He realizes that he is basically giving his father a verbal resume. Even when he is dead, his father still has a way of causing Mitch to feel the need to prove himself. Following the impressive list of accomplishments, he tells his father about Sloane. How he knows his father would approve of her because she is as spirited and stubborn as his old man was. "She is definitely your kind of girl dad."

Happy that he has said all he feels he needs to, Mitch gets to his feet and dusts the dirt and grass clippings from his knees. His attention is drawn to the pile of objects left near the grave, presumably from people who visited in recent weeks. There are old pictures, fake badges, folded pieces of paper which Mitch refuses to read. The one item that draws his stare the most is tucked in the back, barely visible above the grass, the metallic point just barely sticking out. He is careful to not disturb any of the objects as he reaches for the one he wants. Even though he doesn't believe in many of the theories that surround the dead and the people who mourn for them, he doesn't need any more bad karma hanging over his head.

He grabs the warm piece of steel and holds it in his right hand. He knows what it is but finding it sitting here beside his father's tomb is odd. The weight of the object tells him it is definitely not the typical rifle round that hunters use in the woods in these parts. This is a sniper round, and military grade. The bullet covers the entire length of the sheriff's hand and is every bit as thick as the handle of a screwdriver.

Mitch looks down at the .50 mm round in his hand, wondering who would leave something like this next to his father's grave. There is only one person who he could think of that could possibly have access to this kind of ammunition and would have any reason at all to visit this place. Mitch returns the round to the grass, near the place where he found it. It takes some finesse to get it to stand on end because his hands are now shaking. He is outraged thinking that there should be no reason for that person to be here, visiting his father.

Mitch begins to make his way out of the cemetery, mumbling under his breath as he walks. He is trying to answer the questions that are racing through his mind. Why would he be here? Why would Jesse Meyers visit my father's grave?

Chapter 8

With confused feelings, Mitch heads back to his truck. A part of him, a part he is proud to have been living in for the last few weeks, is excited that he will now get to spend the rest of the day with Sloane. She makes him feel good and his mind is free when he is with her. He can put behind him the stresses of the day or whatever pressure Mayor Billings is currently shoving at him whenever he is with her. A smaller part of his conscience, a part he has tried to keep hidden since the events of Graham Park concluded, is filled with rage and anger.

He has always known that Jesse Meyers was out there somewhere. Mitch had slept easier knowing that the man would not be bold enough to show his face around Twisted Timbers after what happened. Now, not only did the man return to town, but he was up on stage, right in front of the camera, practically mocking the sheriff. There is no doubt in his mind that Jesse is the one who left the sniper round sitting at his father's grave, meaning the man has no intention of trying to remain hidden.

He begins driving to his apartment, anxious to see Sloane's reaction when she realizes they will indeed get to spend the day together like they had originally planned. His old truck lets out an odd coughing sound and Mitch sees a small cloud of smoke exit through the exhaust. He thinks to himself that this old beast may have burned through its final quart of oil. The truck has been the only vehicle he has owned since turning sixteen and getting his license, but he had maintained it well, even if the thing was highly battered even before he bought it. His mind drifts back to the mayor and the new Lexus he was driving. The expensive Lexus he was driving. How can the mayor afford such an expensive vehicle? He hadn't really thought about the expensive car in the moments right after it nearly ran him off the road.

Sure, Harry Billings had started a shipping business years ago, but it is a laughing stock around town. It is common knowledge that the business fails to return a profit almost every year. Some folks will tell you that he only started the company because it gave him reasons to play with big trucks and that Billings had never really grown up. Others in town claim that the man wanted to stake claim to the large plot of land that has been in the Billings family for centuries, kind of a nest egg for when the senior Billings passes away.

Another cough of the exhaust pulls Mitch away from his thoughts. He manages to make the right-hand turn into the parking lot of his apartment complex, coasting to a stop near the front door. As he shuts off the engine, a larger cloud of smoke rises from the back of the truck. Mitch gets out and slams the door shut, walks around the back of the truck, pretending to know what he is looking for or what could be causing the issue. The fact of the matter is, he couldn't tell you the difference between a water pump and an alternator, but he wants to make it seem like he knows what he's doing, just in case any of his nosy neighbors happened to see the smoke rise as he pulled in. Failing to see any obvious reason why the truck would be acting up, other than the fact that the machine was built when his father was in high school, he gives a tire a kick and heads inside.

As he enters his apartment, his senses are suddenly overwhelmed. There is loud music blaring from the Bluetooth speaker on the kitchen counter, mixed with the low hum of a vacuum cleaner. The air is filled with a mixture of magnolias and the smell of campfire, two scents Mitch has gotten used to lately. The smell of the burning wood is the latest aroma that Sloane insists all her candles smell like. He notices two of them burning in the small living room. The magnolia scent belongs to the air freshener that she sprays around the apartment whenever she gets in one of her cleaning moods.

As he walks the narrow hallway to their room, he is careful to not make too much noise. He likes it when he can sneak up on her. He had watched her secretly, several times in fact, before they had ever started this relationship. Mitch peeks his head around the corner and watches her as she runs the vacuum along the side of their bed. She is swinging her hips from side to side in rhythm with the music, some rap song from a couple of decades ago that Mitch vaguely recognizes. She is wearing his old Oregon Ducks shirt, and it swings from side to side to match the sway of her body. He loves when she wears his old shirts. The way they fall over her waist, allowing Sloane to show off the legs she has worked so hard on sculpting.

He watches in silence as she turns off the vacuum and begins wrapping up the cord. She has yet to notice him when she spins around and sees him still standing in the doorway of their room. She yelps a bit and gasps for air, startled by his presence. Mitch is the first to speak, albeit in the worst Simon Cowell impersonation ever. "That was bloody brilliant!" he proclaims.

Her cheeks instantly turn pink, teetering on the verge of full-blown red. Her surprised look fades as she slowly makes her way over to him, her eyes never leaving his. For a moment, Mitch braces his abdomen for a swift punch to the gut, a punch that never comes. Instead, she wraps her arms around his neck and gives him a long, slow kiss. The kind of kiss that women use to let the man know that they want more than just a kiss. Mitch has had to learn the hard way about the ways of women, having no real men in his life to teach him about these things. He bends slightly, placing his hands on the backs of her thighs, and lifts her into the air. The kiss lasts for several seconds, Sloane being the first to break contact.

She wiggles away enough to let Mitch know that she wants down, and when he softly puts her back on the floor, she stares at him intently. "You don't think a good girl like me will let you into my pants without a proper dinner, do ya?"

Mitch can do nothing else but chuckle, which earns him the punch in the gut that he was expecting seconds earlier.

"I don't know why you're laughing Mister. I am a sophisticated woman, and I deserve a proper meal," she says to him, half-jokingly.

"Alright, alright. Get dressed and I'll take you to the finest restaurant in all of Twisted Timbers. Only the best for my princess." Mitch is more than willing to play along in her little charade, especially after a kiss like that one.

Sloane lets out a tiny squeal of excitement and races to the closet to find the proper attire. Mitch sits patiently on the bed and waits for her to get ready, still in amazement that she can go from cleaning woman, to Belle of the Ball in less than ten minutes. He tells her that his truck is acting up and they will have to take her car. He says this with hesitation in his voice. He hates when they drive her car, a lime green Volkswagen bug. It's not the there is anything wrong with the car, it's just that he feels like people see him in it and start pointing and laughing. It's probably all in his head, but right now, the green bug is the only transportation they have.

Sloane tosses him the keys and declares herself ready to go. She has pulled on a tiny pair of jean shorts and a maroon tank top. Her blonde hair is pulled back and tucked into a Ducks hat, one of Mitch's Ducks hats. They leave the apartment and less than five minutes later are pulling into the finest restaurant in all of Twisted Timbers, Maddie's Diner.

Chapter 9

Sloane orders the cheeseburger and French fries, the same thing she gets almost every time they come to the diner. Mitch has the country fried steak, tonight's special. As the waitress leaves to give their order to the cook, Sloane reaches her hand across the table and grabs Mitch's. He looks at her, her bright smile framed by the brim of the hat. He smiles back, although if he were being honest, he was feeling a bit uncomfortable. This was the first time that they have been seen together in public when at least one of them wasn't in uniform.

"Mitch, I do believe we are officially a couple. We are on an actual date in public." She winks at him to let him know she knew full well what was racing through his mind. "Are you alright? Do I need to come over there and give you mouth to mouth?"

"I hadn't really thought about this being our first time in public out of uniform until you said that," he lies. The fact is he felt the stares from the other people in the diner, and they hit him harder than the looks he was getting while riding in the passenger seat of her green convertible bug.

"Mitch Thompson, you expect me to believe that? I might have been born at night, but it wasn't last night. I could tell the way you sort of clammed up when we sat down." She squeezes his hand a little tighter and winks at him once more.

"I'm perfectly fine, but I think you might have something in your eye. The left one keeps blinking out of time with the other one." A nervous chuckle escapes his lips before he has the mind to stop it. "In fact, I plan on parading you around town when we're done with dinner. I want the whole town to see how lucky I am."

"Aw, that's sweet," Sloane replies, "but this town aint very big. I'm sure all three hundred or so residents will all be on to us before you even pay the check."

Mitch nods in agreement as the waitress brings their food and sits it on the table. He waits for her to leave before turning back to Sloane, "I went and saw my dad today, at the cemetery." He hadn't really expected to bring it up during dinner, but he wanted her to know that there was more on his mind other than this being their first time in public.

"Mitch, you should have told me, I would have come with you." The disappointment in her face is visible. "I'm sure it wasn't easy being there alone."

His eyes are now focused on his plate, not wanting to get into a discussion about feelings and loss. Thompson men have never been very keen on talking about emotions. "I didn't bring it up because I wanted to talk about him or my feelings, but I found something odd out there."

At first, he noticed the slouch in her shoulders. She had obviously been intrigued by the idea of digging deeper into his mind. When he mentioned finding something at the grave, she perked back up and put her burger down on the plate. She sat at the edge of her seat, her eyes fixed on his.

"There were several bouquets of flowers and other things to remember my father, but underneath them all, I found a sniper round. A large caliber sniper round." He pauses briefly to gauge the surprise in her reaction, she was shocked. "It looked military to me, not that I'm an expert or anything. I know you didn't come to town until after the Graham Park thing, but I would bet money that Jesse is the one who left it there."

"Oh, the famous Jesse Meyers. Isn't that the guy you saw on the television and went chasing this morning?" The excitement in her voice is palpable, causing her to squeal slightly with every word.

"Yes. That's the same guy. He saved my life back at the amusement park, but he is also responsible for several murders that night. I think he is the head of the security detail for Ms. Reynolds." Once again Mitch stops long enough to shovel a large chunk of his meal into his mouth, and steal a glance at Sloane, who is listening intently. "What has me puzzled is why he would leave something at my father's grave? What right does he have to be there at all?"

She ponders the question for a moment, taking the free time to dip a few fries into ketchup, before responding. "Well from what you told me, he is a solid patriot, never having killed an American, at least one that didn't deserve it. Maybe he felt bad that he was unable to stop the killing of your father and wanted to say he was sorry."

"Maybe. It just infuriates me to no end that he was there. I still consider him to be partially responsible for the events that took place that night. He was a willing and active participant. He had no right to visit my father."

"I get what you're saying, I really do. I think it's very peculiar, but I don't think it should bother you who visits your father. I think it is bothering you more that you were unable to talk to this Jesse Meyers today." Sloane is now picking at the remnants of her burger, pulling off the pickles and tossing them in her mouth. "By the way, you really have no proof that it was him who left it there. It could have been anyone. Lord knows this world is filled with whackos and attention seekers, and I'm sure what happened that night was all over the news. Hell, I even saw it down in Los Angeles."

Mitch rubs his hands together, not really happy with her explanation. He knows who left the bullet, and there is no changing his mind. He wants to enjoy this day with Sloane, the last they will have before the busiest weekend of the year and the end of season parade. He loves her, even if he can't remember if he has told her lately.

"Here comes the bill, Mitch. You pay the tab and I'm going to head to the bathroom, I had one too many iced teas. What's next on this first official date for us?" She stares at him as she begins to slide out of the booth.

He hadn't really thought about what they would do after dinner, but now that she is obviously expecting him to figure out the rest of the evening, he quickly says the first thing that comes to mind. "I thought I would make you hate the game of golf, at least the putting portion of golf. I thought we would play a round at Wild Beavers Golf 'N Gulp."

Her eyes brighten instantly, which they do every time her competitiveness is tested. "I will stomp you. I probably haven't told you this, but I almost went pro when I was seven." She was almost able to get out the full sentence before breaking out in laughter.

"They have a professional league for mini-golf? I think you're full of shit is what I think. Care to make the round a little more interesting?" Mitch loves to test her patience and scratch at her competitive streak, one that is only matched by that of Mitch himself.

"A bet? As long as you are going to pay up. I love a bet." She is now seated beside him on the same side of the booth. If there were any questions by the few residents in the diner as to what the two officers were up to, that question has now been answered.

"I say, the loser of the round has to buy the drinks tonight at the Bottom Dollar." The bar had been a favorite of his before he became accustomed to racing home to spend more time with her. She has often bragged about her ability to drink, but he has yet to see her in action.

"I got a better idea, that is if you're feeling confident. I say the loser not only buys drinks, but since it is a Thursday night, and I know what happens at the bar on Thursday nights, the loser also has to sing a karaoke song." She wraps her tanned arms around his neck and leans in to him, challenging him with her eyes. "Or are you chicken."

Mitch leans back slightly from her, just enough that he has regained use of his hands. He extends the right one to her, "you have yourself a deal. It's on like Donkey Kong."

Chapter 10

It feels like he has been sitting in this chair for days between the pain in his hands, the evil stare from the large stranger sitting across from him and the bouts of falling in and out of consciousness. He still has no idea why these men have come into his home and began torturing him, but Mr. Billings has surmised that his son has gotten into some serious trouble and he is the one to blame for this. He wonders how much longer this ordeal is going to last as he contemplates ways in which he might be able to talk himself out of this predicament.

The large Mexican is still sitting silently on the couch across the living room, his dark eyes fixed permanently on the old man. He is solid from head to toe and has barely moved a muscle in the time he has been nestled in the soft cushions. Mr. Billings can't see a gun or weapon of any sort on the man, but that doesn't help give him any false hope that he will be able to physically escape the house. He is far older and much smaller than the other man to even entertain any notion that he would be able to overpower him.

The longer the old man is forced to sit in this chair, in the same position, the more and more his body feels worse than it does normally. The rope isn't tied around his body so tight that it is squeezing him or making his breathing uncomfortable, but his joints ache and his head is beginning to pound. He thinks about asking the larger man for something to drink but refrains from it. He just wants to sit here quietly and keep the man as far away from his chair as possible.

The big man said someone wanted to come talk to him, El Carnicero, not that the ex-teacher has any idea what that name means. This man will surely be in charge of the other two men and must certainly be willing to listen to reason. The old man begins to think this will be his best chance to get out of here without being harmed. Well, without being harmed any further. He has been an English teacher his entire adult life, surely, he will be able to use the skills he has learned to persuade the leader to let him go.

He is surprised at how little his hands hurt. The knives went straight through his palms and he can see the holes in his flesh as he looks down at them. If he were a religious man, he would find the irony in how his hands must resemble those of the crucified son of Mary and Joseph. Dorothy would have noticed the similarity right away, although she wasn't a firm believer until after her diagnosis.

As soon as the old man closes his eyes, giving in to the feeling of helplessness, he quickly reopens them at the sound of his front door opening. The night sky has fallen, and the large Mexican man had failed to turn on any lights in the house, making it difficult at first to see the faces of the two men that entered the house. His eyes painfully try to adjust to the brightness of the lights as they are turned on. He recognizes the smaller man entering the living room, he was the one that jabbed the knives into his hands. He was also the only man to speak to him when they were here earlier, but now, he just enters the room and stands in the corner next to his brother.

The new man that strolls confidently into the room, walking as if he is taking his turn down the runway, looks around the room, taking in the pictures on the walls and the books on the table next to the chair. His suit is meticulous, and every finger of his hand is dressed in bulky jewelry. The man is obviously used to being the center of attention whenever he enters a room and this instance is no different. He relishes the attention and the fear that he sees in the eyes of the people he encounters, the senior Mr. Billings being no different.

The old man shows no fear. He has no idea who this man is nor does he know why he is here. It's not that Mr. Billings is braver than he should be in his current predicament. His lack of fear comes more from the fact that there is nothing he can do about whatever is about to happen. Even with the thickness of tension that is resonating in the room, the old man can't help but think about the last words he read in the Stephen King book, 'shit don't mean shit', and there isn't much he can do about this shit.

Finally, the boss stops in front of the old man and begins to speak. "First, allow me to introduce myself. The people call me El Carnicero, do you know what that means old man?"

Mr. Billings struggles to speak, the dryness of his mouth more prevalent now than ever. Words refuse to exit so he simply shakes his head.

The man looks down on the prisoner, grins slightly and says, "The Butcher."

Chapter 11

The round of golf was far less exciting than Mitch had hoped for. If Sloane had joined the mythical professional mini-golf tour, there is no doubt in his mind that she would have been a champion. He never stood a chance. As they wait in line for ice cream, Mitch sees the mayor drive by in his shiny luxury car, the one that looks far too expensive for the mayor of a small town like this to be driving.

"Hey, let me ask you a question. How much do you think the mayor makes?" He knows that Sloane has about as much knowledge regarding the salary of the mayor as he does, but he hopes he can zero in on a ballpark figure. "That's him in that silver Lexus that's at the corner. Do you think it's a little out of his pay range?"

Sloane looks over her right shoulder, to where the Lexus is now making the turn. "I guess so, but doesn't he own some kind of shipping business? Maybe that's where he got the money to pay for the car." She looks away from Mitch after saying this, bends a little and asks the teenager behind the counter for a soft serve cone with rainbow sprinkles, Mitch opts for a chocolate malt. They finish off their treats sitting on a bench under a large oak tree, in a grassy area that has been vacant of buildings for as long as Mitch can remember.

At the urging from Mitch, Sloane agrees to leave the green bug parked and the couple walk hand in hand to the Bottom Dollar Saloon. It's only a couple of blocks away and the sun disappeared behind the trees hours ago, cooling off another humid late-summer day in Oregon. They banter back and forth, mostly about how lopsided the scores had been on the golf course. Mitch has never been what you would call a gracious loser, but with her, he is a completely different man. He likes the playful ribbing she gives him, the teasing that comes with every embarrassing loss she hands him.

The setting sun has laid an orange blanket on the streets of the town, many of the store front windows glistening with the few rays of light that manage to sneak their way through the branches. There is more traffic now than when they left the diner, the early birds have begun to flock into town. Mitch is comfortable, surprisingly, walking with Sloane through the streets of town, not caring who sees them or what the residents might be saying behind their backs. He likes this woman, and this is what normal people who are involved in a relationship do, or at least he thinks it is.

As they near the entrance to the bar, Sloane bumps into him playfully. He looks at her from the corner of his eyes and sees her pursed lips, her soft but full lips. "So, Sheriff, what song are you going to sing for me tonight?"

He holds the door and she shuffles past him. He had somewhat forgotten about the bet they had made, and while he is more than happy to do the gentlemanly thing and buy the drinks, getting up to sing a song is not his idea of a good time. "I have no idea," he murmurs as he files through the door behind her.

They find a couple of stools near the middle of the bar, the stage directly behind them. It's still early, so there's a limited number of people inside. The DJ is still setting up his equipment and has yet to begin playing any music or calling people up to sing. Mitch orders a beer and scans the room for faces that he knows, for people who are likely to give him a hard time after hearing him sing. Sloane speaks to the bartender, a mountain of a man with slicked back hair and a t-shirt on that is at least two sizes too small. Mitch rubs Sloane's back while she places her order, letting the man behind the bar know that she is taken, no matter how much testosterone he has pumping through his bulging muscles.

Once the bartender leaves to get their drinks, Mitch turns in his stool to look directly at her. "I really don't know how the mayor could afford a car like that. You're not from around here so you have no idea. His transportation company has always been a laughing stock. The old-timers say that he only started the company so his father, my high school English teacher, wouldn't force him to go to college."

Mitch stops talking long enough for the bartender to place the drinks in front of them. He hands the behemoth his credit card and asks him to leave the tab running. Mitch grabs his Miller Lite and looks down at the assortment of things that were left in front of Sloane. She reaches for the salt shaker and lemon, which were brought to go with her double shot of tequila. He watches in amazement as she licks the salt from her hand, throws back the drink and puts the lemon in her mouth, her face never showing a single sign of remorse. She slowly places the remains of the lemon inside the shot glass and reaches for the tumbler of bourbon that remains. Apparently, Mitch thinks to himself, drinking is something else that Sloane is far better at than he is.

"I understand what you're saying, but maybe he does a little better with his business than the town gives him credit for. I'm not sure I understand why it matters to you." She sips on the bourbon while waiting for his response.

"I'm not sure that it bothers me, it's just that, everything that man does gets under my skin. Did you ever meet someone and everything they do just bothers you?"

Sloane thinks about the question briefly, "you mean other than you?"

"Let's just forget it. I probably wouldn't even have noticed if he didn't damn near run me over and honk at me. When did you become such a drinker?" Mitch downs the last of his beer and orders another. If he is going to get up on stage and sing, it's probably a good idea to add some liquid encouragement first.

"You know my dad was a cop, and my brother. I've spent many a night in bars with cops. When you're the daughter of a cop who passes away, you get free shots without even having to ask for them." She takes another sip of bourbon, allowing it to sit in her mouth long enough to savor the flavor. "I don't drink nearly as much or as often as I used to, but every drink I have now will make you sound even better when you get up and sing."

Chapter 12

An hour has passed since they ordered their first drinks and the bar is starting to fill up. Mitch has not recognized anyone who has walked in, meaning they are all tourists who will be gone by Sunday, people the sheriff will never have to look in the eye again. He's had four beers and is working on his fifth, while Sloane has had a second shot of tequila but is still nursing the same glass of bourbon. A slightly overweight redhead named Candy is currently giving her finest rendition of a Madonna song, with every high note she hits perfectly, Mitch is feeling more and more pressure.

"I think it's about your turn," Sloane declares as she tosses back the last of the bourbon in the glass and waves her hand in a circular motion to the bartender, the international sign for another round. Mitch watches her as she gets down from the barstool and walks over the edge of the stage. He has no idea what she is up to, but she loves the way she confidently strides across the room. She talks to the man playing the music for a few seconds, stopping once to turn and point to Mitch. He tries to not pay attention but the nerves he is feeling makes that hard to do.

She returns, sits back down and sips on her freshly refilled bourbon. Mitch waits for her to speak, but she says nothing. She just looks straight ahead, refusing to look at him or even acknowledge his presence. "Aren't you going to tell me what I'll be singing?"

"I thought I would keep it a surprise, but I'll give you a hint. It's the only song I've heard you sing where you knew all the words." She speaks confidently and with a hint of teasing in her voice. Before Mitch has time to respond, he hears the DJ announcing to the growing crowd that a new singer is coming up, and that he is the Sheriff of this lovely town.

Mitch downs the last of his beer and grabs another before going up to the stage. If it were anyone else who had manipulated the situation to get him up here with a microphone in his hand, he would have been able to say no to them. Sloane, on the other hand, makes him a better man, even if it does come along with a few things he swore he would never do, including karaoke.

He keeps his eyes on her and she waves to him from the bar. The lights are bright in his face, making it hard to see the lyrics that will scroll down the screen positioned in the corner of the elevated platform. He hears the familiar music of a Randy Travis song, the first song he remembered hearing his dad sing when they were driving in the truck. He does his best to sound like he's not nervous, belting out every word right on cue, without having to look at the lyrics even once. By the time he hits the second chorus and the repetitive forever and ever amens that come at the end, he is almost enjoying being up here. Almost. The bright light in his face drowns out most of the crowd but he can see the glistening smile from Sloane at the bar, and that's all he needs.

The song ends, and he quickly jumps down from the stage and races back to the bar. A fresh beer is waiting on him, apparently from a stranger in the corner according to the bartender. Mitch looks around and allows Sloane to poke a little fun at him, teasing that he must have a groupie already. There is still no one in the bar that he recognizes, a point that Mitch is thankful for after his performance.

He begins sipping the beer before turning to her, "how did you know that I knew the words to that song?"

"You hum it all the time, usually you don't even know that you're doing it. I took a chance and it paid off so well you even got a free beer out of it. Who knew someone else would like it as much as I did?" She throws back another shot of tequila, this time she doesn't bother with the messiness of the salt or the lemon slice.

Mitch hadn't felt the person sit down at the bar on the opposite side of him, his back was turned to everyone else in the bar other than Sloane. He felt a slight nudge on his shoulder, which interrupted his admiration for the woman who drinks like a sailor but looks like a runway model. He turns slowly, thinking someone just bumped into him while trying to get a drink at the bar, when he is met face to face with the man he last saw in person at Graham Park, and the same man that was on his television earlier in the day. Sitting next to him, in dark sunglasses and a black hat is Jesse Meyers, at least that's the name he went by back then.

"That was a solid performance, Sheriff, and a classic song choice. You can't go wrong with Randy Travis." Jesse is staring straight ahead, not even bothering to look at Mitch as he speaks.

"You have some nerve showing your face around here, let alone sitting down here and speaking to me. I should arrest you right now." Mitch can feel his face turning red with every word.

"Calm down, you could arrest me, but it would get you nowhere. The name you know me by doesn't exist and the name I'm using is perfectly clean. If the F.B.I. and every other agency hasn't had any luck, I doubt a small-town cop will do much better pinning anything on me." He stops and takes a long swallow from his beer, one of those craft beers that Mitch hates and the choice in beverage causes Mitch to dislike this man even more. Sheriff Thompson is strictly a Miller Lite guy and subscribes completely to the theory that if something isn't broke, why try to fix it or make it better, especially when it comes to beer.

"Maybe I'll just drag you out in the street and shoot you. Isn't that what people like you do?" The sheriff is stumbling over his words, anger getting the best of him. His back is turned to Sloane, but he can feel her leaning against him trying to hear every word.

"Look Mitch, I didn't plan on seeing you in here tonight. I looked for your truck in the parking lot and didn't see it. If I knew you were here, I wouldn't have come in. I'm only in town as long as it takes for Ms. Reynolds to finish her business."

"My truck is having issues. We drove Sloane's," Mitch pauses briefly to consider his word choice before proceeding. "We drove her vehicle tonight." There's no need to give Jesse more reason to look down on him by saying they walked from down the road because Mitch doesn't like to be seen driving in a green Volkswagen.

"Like I said, once Mayor Billings and Ms. Reynolds make everything official, we will get out of your hair. I don't like being back here anymore than you want me here."

Mitch is aware of the business of Ms. Reynolds and her company, but he has no idea what Mayor Billings has to do with it. For as long as he can remember the title of mayor was, more or less, just so the council members had a face of the town. Someone to wave to guests as they arrived. The council is who makes all the laws and grants the permits to anyone wanting to build, especially anyone wanting to build something as large as a resort.

"You say Ms. Reynolds has business with Mayor Billings? Do you know what it is?" The talk of the mayor has loosened the noose around his neck, the one that tightened the instant he noticed Jesse sitting next to him.

"Mayor Billings is selling my employer the land he owns, to use for her development. They are supposed to sign the contract in the next couple of days." Jesse nonchalantly raises his arm and another dark lager is brought to him.

"That would explain where he got the money to drive around in that fancy car. Thanks for clearing that up for me." Mitch turns to look at Sloane, but only long enough to roll his eyes so she knows he is agitated with the man sitting next to him.

Jesse sits quietly for a second before replying, "he might have a fancy car, but it has nothing to do with my employer or their deal. No funds have been transferred as of yet. He was driving that Lexus when he showed up to greet us when we got to town a few days ago." He puts his beer down and swivels in his stool, this time looking Mitch straight in the face. "In fact, the real reason I came over here is to tell you that things in town may not be what they appear. Ms. Reynolds has asked me to look into your mayor and I have found some interesting things."

Mitch contemplates this for a moment, Mayor Billings has never been the kind of person Mitch liked, but he also never considered him as a danger to the town. "I'd love to know what you found out, or at least what you think you've found. Care to enlighten me, I mean I am just a small-town cop."

"I don't have much hard evidence, Mitch, but I did see some familiar faces in town the last couple of days. The kind of guys that no town needs around. I would bet that they are involved with the mayor in some capacity, and if they are, there is going to be problems. Big problems."

"Who are these people? Friends of yours?" First the mayor and now there are strangers in town that Jesse considers dangerous. "This is an important weekend for this town, especially after everything that has gone on this year."

"The Arroyo brothers are in town. I've seen them with my own eyes at least twice. They work for El Carnicero, The Butcher, and they are not very nice guys. I doubt they are here for the peace and quiet."

Mitch sits on the edge of his seat, listening intently, half believing what he is being told and half trying to debunk it. "The Arroyo brothers huh? The Butcher? Are you sure you haven't had too much to drink tonight Jesse, or whatever your name is?"

"It's Ethan. Ethan Ward. I know what I saw Mitch, and if these guys are in town, then things are going to get very intense around here. All I'm asking is that you do your due diligence and check them out. El Carnicero is not the guy you want to have poking around, there's a reason he is called The Butcher. He makes Pablo look like a big softie." Ethan, or Jesse, throws a twenty on the bar and gets off his stool. He begins to walk away from Mitch and stops. "If my hunches are right, and they usually are, the Arroyo boys are here for one thing. I'm guessing that one thing is directly related to Mayor Billings. I've had a bad feeling about ole Harry since the moment I met him."

The familiar stranger turns and exits the bar, not even pausing to look back to Mitch. The two men talked for nearly fifteen minutes and in that time, Ethan didn't even acknowledge Sloane or the fact that she was sitting there, listening to every word. Mitch is clearly shaken, his hands trembling, and Sloane is starting to feel the effects of too much clear liquor. The two pay their tab and rise together and exit the bar.

"Where's my car? Oh yeah, you might have to help me walk down to the diner." Her words are slurring a bit.

"I got you. Let's get you home and into bed." Mitch tucks his arm around her waist, a motion she finds hysterical for a reason only known to her. They walk side by side down the street, Sloane laughing violently the whole time. She is apparently the type of person who finds everything funny when they've had a little extra. Mitch, on the other hand, sobered up completely the minute Jesse Meyers sat down next to him. Now his mind is racing with possible reasons why the Arroyo brothers and El Carnicero would be in town and what kind of mess the mayor has gotten involved in.

It takes a little effort to get Sloane into the passenger seat of the tiny car, and even more finesse to get her out when they reach the apartment parking lot. She is a small woman which allows Mitch to throw her over his shoulder and carry her through the front door. She manages to make her way to the bedroom on her own, and Mitch heads for the bathroom. By the time he finishes his business, he finds her in the bed and sprawled across the middle of it sideways. She has managed to remove her clothes, all of her clothes, before collapsing on top of the comforter. He struggles to roll her over and position her body under the blanket and climbs in beside her. He kisses the back of her shoulder before turning off the light and putting his head on his pillow.

Kevin M. Moehring

Chapter 13

The old man sits with his eyes closed, pondering the name of the man in front of him, the man in charge of his captivity. There is only one normal reason why the people would call him The Butcher, and this man looks nothing like a person who slaughters cows for a living. He has obviously gotten his name from horrible acts he has committed to the people who have gotten on his bad side, one way or another. This doesn't bode well for the old man ever getting out of this situation.

His moment of realization is broken by the voice of the slender man, who has turned to his two employees and has begun speaking rapidly in Spanish. He has no idea what the conversation is about, but only one man is speaking. When the living room becomes silent again, the old man watches the larger of the two brothers hurry out of the room toward the kitchen. He returns with a glass of water and feeds it to the old man. The feeling of the water coating his parched throat is better than Mr. Billings could have expected.

His panic and fear subside momentarily, thinking the boss has realized there must be some mistake and they have captured the wrong man. This moment of relief is short lived, stripped from him when The Butcher has seen enough and ends the rehydration with a strong slap to the back of the head of the bulky Mexican. The force of the attack is strong enough to make the man spill the remaining contents of the glass all over the old man. The sizable man sets the now empty glass on the side table and returns to his post on the couch.

"Now that you have had a drink, are you able to talk to me?"

The old man swallows several times before trying to reply. "I think I can talk. I tried to tell these brutes that you obviously have the wrong man."

"Yes. I am aware. We are searching for a Mr. Harry Billings. I did not know that you have the same name as your son, and that is most unfortunate for you."

"Now that you know, are you going to let me go?" The old man is hopeful but not overly optimistic. A man doesn't get a name like that by being fair.

The Butcher chuckles and throws his head back. He stops laughing abruptly and looks down on the old man again. "It was unfortunate that my brutes, as you call them, made the mistake of thinking you were the man we were looking for. Your son has chosen to steal from me and that can't be overlooked. As you can clearly see, I am not the kind of man you steal from."

Tears begin to form in the eyes of the old man, "any issues you have with my son is between the two of you. I'm not sure what I have to do with it."

"I wish I could say that I agree with you, old man, but now you have seen our faces. Besides, I think your son may need some visual evidence as to why you should never steal from The Butcher." The way the boss says his own name, as if the word was spelled with multiple o's instead of the singular u, makes the title sound more ominous.

The smaller of the two brothers makes his way over to where The Butcher had been standing. The man hands a small leather pouch to his boss, who unfolds it on the side table, right on top of the Stephen King novel. The senior Billings tries to avert his eyes from the contents of the pouch, but he can't resist looking. Like a military field surgeon, The Butcher runs his fingers along the assortment of stainless-steel tools, each resting in its appropriate slot in the pouch. He looks at the prisoner, obviously sizing him up and returns his gaze to the tools before finally selecting one.

The Butcher turns his back to the old man, never revealing which instrument he has chosen. The old man is now crying, loudly, and is not trying to hide it. He mumbles under his breath, repeating the words "Dorothy, I love you." He says the words over and over as he watches every movement of the killer in front of him.

The Butcher is standing still, arms in front of him, facing away from the old man. He too is mumbling words under his breath. "If you take from me, I take from you." He recites the line several times before falling silent, taking in a deep breath and turning quickly on his heels. The boss looks to the smaller of the two men sitting on the couch, who pulls out his cell phone. Within seconds, loud music begins to fill the room.

The music is dark, ominous, with low rumbles from a bass drum and high-pitched squeals from a mandolin. The Mexican killer is moving his body to the sound of the song, never turning around to look at his target. The old man in the chair is so caught up in the movements of The Butcher that he doesn't even notice the larger man return to his post behind the chair until he feels the firm grip on his neck once again, and the second hand placed against his forehead. The strength of the man has forced Mr. Billings to look at what El Carnicero is doing, but more importantly, what he is about to do.

Without another word and with exact precision, The Butcher raises the shiny knife which turns out to be less than intimidating. The surgeon's weapon has a small but razor-sharp blade and the man swings it through the air in rhythm with the music. As the tempo in the instrumental piece begins to speed up, so does the movements of the man with the knife. The Mexican killer spins multiple times and finally faces the man in the chair.

Like a stripper on stage, the killer times each step he takes to the melodic cymbals that pierce through the small cell phone speaker. His lanky body moves in ways that make him look more like a newborn giraffe rather than a man feared around the world for his ruthless nature. He puts one foot in front of the other, in a slow march, until he is standing right in front of the bound man, whose bowels have let go in a warm stream that ends on the worn-out carpet. The music stops abruptly, the only sound that can be heard now is the rapid breathing from Mr. Billings as the killer leans in close to him. The old man can smell the mustiness of old cigar smoke that emanates from the designer suit the killer wears.

"When you feel the pain, I want you to remember who did this to you. Your son is responsible for everything that is about to happen," the man whispers. "He made a deal and chose to steal from me instead. Now he has to learn what happens when you fuck with The Butcher." Once again, he elongates the word, using the double o sound.

The old man feels the hands on his neck and head tighten even further. His head is pinned to the back of the chair as the killer is only inches away. He closes his eyes, refusing to look at the man who is surely going to kill him. He wants a different image, any image other than the Mexican with the knife, to be the last thing he sees before he dies. He remembers his wife, Dorothy, and the way she looked on their wedding day. The way her hair was pulled back, showing off her glowing smile and the sparkle in her eyes. He retraces her steps in his mind, as she makes her way to the altar. As she takes his hand and squeezes it, assuming her position next to him, the old man snaps back to the present and the piercing pain as the sharp tip of the surgeon's blade begins to cut into his eyelids.

Kevin M. Moehring

Friday

Chapter 14

It is rare for Mitch to wake up and get out of bed before Sloane does. This morning, it doesn't come as a shock to him. She passed out right away last night and since he didn't get much sleep himself, he rarely heard her move around or toss in bed. He showered and dressed, tiptoeing through the room to try not to disturb his sleeping girlfriend. He left a half of pot of coffee for her in the kitchen and left the apartment in silence.

Mitch had forgotten that his truck was broke down when he first left the apartment and instead of leaving Sloane without a vehicle, he decided to walk the three blocks to the station. The sun was just beginning to rise, and the dense fog and chilly moisture of the cool morning showers the town in a gray foam. The streets are quiet, it is far too early for any of the visitors to be awake and exploring the town. Looking up and down the streets, Mitch can almost see why Sloane usually gets up this early and goes running every morning. Almost.

The sheriff didn't sleep very much last night. His mind was racing with thoughts of the Arroyo brothers, The Butcher and Mayor Billings. On top of those things, he still couldn't get Jesse Meyers out of his mind. The bravado of the man to walk right up to him at the bar and carry on a conversation, as if he wasn't a highly sought-after fugitive, leaves the sheriff perplexed. Mitch is kicking himself for not calling the F.B.I. and having Jesse, or Ethan Ward, arrested and taken to prison.

He easily takes the steps into the concrete building two at a time, swinging the large glass door open with ease. He strolls into the office and is met with the smiling face of Stuart Johnson, perched at his desk and raising his eyes to meet Mitch's. The elder officer stands and follows Mitch into the sheriff's office.

"Good morning Sheriff, I have some coffee made if you're interested."

"I had some before leaving the house. I have a few things I need you to get me information on. I met our friend Jesse last night and he gave me some names of people he has seen in town. I'm not sure how much of his story I believe, but I want to know as much as I can on the people he mentioned."

Stuart looks at the sheriff with a concerned look, his lips lowering at the corners. "You actually had a talk with Jesse Meyers? Why didn't you arrest him?"

"We were at the Bottom Dollar. I couldn't decide if I should finish my beer before or after I slapped the cuffs on him."

Stuart chuckles at this, the laugh going on a little longer than is comfortable for either man. "Ah, the now infamous karaoke. I watched the video on the computer, you weren't half bad."

It's hard for Mitch to hide his anger and surprise. He had thought only the people seated in the bar would have seen his performance. He is not what you would call a whore to technology, one of the people who keep up with all the latest gadgets and would rather spend two weeks' pay on a new cell phone than a decent wardrobe, but he remembers Sloane telling him over and over that you can find anything you want on the internet.

"Sorry Mitch, just having a little fun. What did our friend have to say?" Stuart sensed the unease in the sheriff and being a person that never wants to make waves, quickly tries to change the subject.

"He's going by the name of Ethan Ward now, working for Cassie Reynolds as the head of her security. He said he saw a few faces around town that he recognizes, the Arroyo brothers. These guys are apparently bad business and work for a man from Mexico, some drug lord named The Butcher, but Jesse used the Spanish word for it."

"El Carnicero?" Stuart chimed in.

"Yeah that's it. How did you know that?" Mitch is surprised that Stuart has any knowledge of foreign languages.

"I've heard the guy's name before, seen a few articles online about him. He is a bad character. Rumor has it he has a collection of body parts in glass jars sitting on his desk. This guy makes Hannibal Lecter look like a misguided chef." The nervousness in Stuart's voice is apparent, his hands rubbing his thighs to dry the sweat that has begun to form.

"See what you can find on them and bring it to me. I'm not very good on the internet thing. Jesse seems to think these guys are here in town and it has something to do with Mayor Billings. By the way, do you know what kind of car the mayor drives?"

"He has the old Ford truck, the blue one."

"That's what I thought too, Stuart, but yesterday he damn near ran me off the road in a shiny Lexus. How do you think he can afford something like that?"

Stuart pauses for a moment, "Honestly, I have no idea. We all know his trucking company is just a front and doesn't really make any money. I can't believe that the role of mayor pays all that well."

"That's what I was thinking, but if these hitmen are in town, and somehow linked to the mayor, that could explain the new-found money. I don't like where this is going, so I want to get out in front of it if we can."

"Copy that, Sheriff. I'll dig up what I can on these guys and get it to you as soon as possible." Stuart turns and begins to leave the room. He turns back to the sheriff as if he has more to say but thinks better of it.

"What is it Stu?" the sheriff urges.

"You really weren't bad last night. Karaoke is something I never thought I would see you do. I like the effect Sloane is having on you. We have both been through some crazy stuff this last year, I'm glad to see you actually living your life. Lord knows you deserve it."

"Thanks Stuart, but I'm afraid that was a one-time performance. Go see what you can dig up." Sheriff Thompson watches his deputy dutifully return to his desk and type away at his keyboard, albeit with a slight smile on his face.

Chapter 15

Mitch has returned his attention to the stack of files on his desk. He is not really focused on the paperwork, thinking more about the names that Ethan Harper had given him the night before, and how or why these men are in town. Every few minutes he steals a glance at Stuart through the large window in his office, in hopes that the deputy will have some new information to share. Time seems to be standing still for the sheriff, which is not normal during the tourist season. He should be focused on more important things that require his attention, like traffic control or getting the barricades in position for the parade on Sunday.

Instinctually, he reaches for his phone, hoping to find a text message from Sloane. She must still be sleeping off the remnants and blurriness of last night. She isn't due into the office until three but it's not like her to still be sleeping at nine. By now she would have normally had her run and showered. He sends her a message and asks how she's doing, hoping it will bring a response sooner rather than later.

No sooner had he set his phone down and the melodic ring startles him. He quickly flips the phone open and answers it without looking at the number of the person calling. His heart drops from his chest, expecting to hear Sloane's voice and being greeted by that of Mayor Billings is more than a little depressing.

"Good morning Sheriff."

"Hello Mayor, what can I do for you?"

"I know you are busy, with the parade and all, but I haven't heard from my father since Wednesday. I was hoping you could send someone out to check on him."

Sheriff Thompson rolls his eyes and holds the phone slightly away from his ear. The mayor is one of those people that talks way to loud for the situation, demanding to be heard over whatever background noise is present. "Is something wrong?"

"How the hell am I supposed to know? Isn't that what you get paid to figure out?" the mayor replies gruffly.

"Mayor, I get paid to keep the town safe, not run out and look in on your father because he hasn't checked in with you lately. That sounds like something his son should do." It's not like Mitch to be combative with anyone, especially the mayor, but the lack of sleep and the sharp tone with which he is being talked to has him on edge.

"Unlike you, I am a very important and busy man. I don't have time to run all the way to the other side of town right now. I have important things to deal with in case you haven't noticed."

"Yes, mayor, I'm sure you do. By the way, why don't you slow down while driving through town. You almost ran me over yesterday." Mitch thinks about bringing up the new sports car but decides not to.

"Like I said, I'm a very busy man. Besides, I'm sure you could probably send your girlfriend out to check on my father, or do you keep her in the office so you can look at that tight body all day?" The mayor laughs loudly, as if he has told the funniest one-liner in history.

Mitch contemplates the best response to what the mayor is insinuating and decides this is not the time to keep bickering. "I'll send someone out there as soon as I can. Is there anything else I can do for you?"

"Not unless you can convince Ms. Reynolds to sign these papers. Ha, who am I kidding, you wouldn't have the slightest idea how to live in my world. It's a little over your pay grade."

"Have a good day mayor, I'll let you know if there is anything wrong with your father. It's been a pleasure as always." Mitch hangs up the phone, not waiting to hear a response from the town leader.

Mitch can feel his blood start to boil. The hairs rising on his arms. How does the mayor have the audacity to talk to him the way he does and why does Mitch not have the strength to stand up to the man? Surely there is something wrong with the mayor talking about Sloane the way he just did. He rubs his hands through his hair and lets out a deep sigh. He practically jumps at the sound of his phone beeping. He reads the message from Sloane and is relieved that she is awake. He sends her a response and puts his phone away in time to see Stuart come walking through his office door.

"Hey Sheriff, I got the information you wanted. Looks like the two men you were asking about are Juan and Humberto Arroyo and they are nasty guys. There are literally dozens of stories of things these guys have done in Mexico, most of which sound like they are straight from a movie. On top of that, they indeed work for a man named The Butcher, real name is unknown, and he is far worse than they are."

"We can do without any of the retelling of the stories. Were you able to find out why they might be here in Twisted Timbers?"

"Nothing from what I can see, although The Butcher is mixed up in just about every form of illegal activity you can think of. Meth, cocaine, guns, explosives and even human trafficking. He is a bad man. A very bad man."

Mitch takes a second to look over some of the papers that Stuart placed on his desk. The articles and photos all point to the violence that surrounds The Butcher and his two thugs. "Let's just work on the assumption that these guys were just passing through town. We have nothing else to go on other than the word of Jesse Meyers, and I'm not sure how much stock we can put on that."

"Sounds good to me Sheriff. I'm not sure if I can take much more excitement around here. I'm really looking forward to a few months of peace and quiet."

"You and me both," the sheriff agrees. "We aren't there yet however. The mayor called and wants someone to check on his father. He says he hasn't heard from him since Wednesday night. Think you can run out there and check things out?"

"Sure. I always liked Mr. Billings. I still can't believe the mayor shares blood with him, they are complete opposites."

"Yeah. I guess the apple might fall a little further from the tree than everyone says. I'm going to stay here, at least until Lucille and Deputy Nichols get in." Mitch had to catch himself from referring to the third deputy as Sloane, something that has become increasingly harder to do. "Once they get here, I may take a trip out to see the mayor myself. I have some things I want to ask him, but I want him to look me in the eyes when he lies to me."

"Sounds good. I'll head to see Mr. Billings now. I'll call if I have any issues." Stuart turns and leaves the sheriff's office, stopping only to grab his hat and jacket

from his own desk before leaving the station through
the front door.

Chapter 16

Left alone in the office, Mitch suddenly feels the ping from his stomach that reminds him he failed to eat breakfast. He looks at his watch and realizes it's almost noon. Sheriff Thompson looks around at the empty station before walking to the breakroom and rummaging through the refrigerator, pushing aside the containers of yogurt, which Sloane eats almost every day, and finds the leftovers from a box lunch he didn't finish a few days ago. After heating the half of a hamburger in the microwave, he returns to his desk and starts reading the articles that Stuart printed out regarding the Mexican men.

He skims the articles mostly, but the headlines grab his attention. Words like mutilated, tortured and dismembered are all used to describe the condition of the bodies which were found and attributed to The Butcher and his men. Mitch thinks that Stuart hit the nail on the head when he described this guy as a very bad man. The pictures that go along with the articles give meaning to the headlines. Bloodied faces, severed arms and gouged eyes seem to be the normal result for anyone who has crossed paths with these men.

He must have been studying the papers longer than he thought, mesmerized by the viciousness of the attacks, because when he looked up from his desk, Lucille Pennington had arrived. She sits in the desk furthest away from the sheriff's office, closest to the front door. The running joke at the station is that Lucille was here when they built the building. She has been around as long as anyone can remember. Her job nowadays consists of answering the phones and deciphering which complaints require the sheriff's attention and which ones can just be filed away.

Mitch feels a little more at ease now that someone else is in the building. The old building has a way of making a person feel like they are being watched or give them an uneasy feeling, as if the building doesn't want them there. Sheriff Thompson sticks his head out to formally greet Lucille before returning to his desk. As he sits down, the office phone rings. He looks up and watches Lucille as she talks and then motions to him that the call is for him.

"Sheriff Thompson, can I help you?"

"Hey Sheriff, it's Stuart. I'm out here at the Billings place. We have a problem." Deputy Johnson is breathing quickly and taking deep gasps between every word.

"What is it? Is Mr. Billings alright?" Mitch rose to his feet the second he heard the rattled tone in the voice of the deputy.

"He's alive. At least for now. He's been attacked."

"What do you mean he's been attacked? He is the nicest guy in town. I see no reason why anyone would want to hurt him."

"I don't know anything about all of that Sheriff. All I know is I'm looking at him and someone has been here and done some damage to the old man."

Mitch can hear Stuart saying words to himself that he must not have intended to say out loud, or else the deputy pulled the phone away from his mouth. "Calm down Stuart, tell me what you see."

"Well, I knocked on the door a few times and didn't get any response. I knew Mr. Billings was here because his car is parked out front. I tried the handle to the door and it was unlocked, so I went in. I called his name a few more times and heard a faint sound from the living room. When I turned the corner, I saw him."

"What did you see? It's important you tell me exactly what you saw and what kind of condition he's in." Mitch is just as startled by the findings, but he has the ability to appear calm and slow his racing heart better than most men.

"Well, it looks like someone came in and put a knife or something sharp through his hands. Kind of pinned him down to the chair that way. There are no blades still stuck in him, but the wounds are pretty obvious. The old man must have been scared out of his mind because he soiled himself."

"Stuart, is he alive? I mean, that sounds awful but from the way you sound I would have thought he was beaten worse than a few knife wounds."

A long pause from the other end of the line. "That's not all sheriff. At first, I didn't see it because his head was slouched, and I couldn't really see his face. When I got closer to try and check for a pulse, that's when I noticed it."

The anticipation and waiting took its toll on the sheriff and he practically screamed at Stuart. "What? What did you see?"

Now the deputy is sniffling, obviously traumatized over what he has seen. "His eyes. They, they cut out his eyes."

Chapter 17

It took several minutes, but Mitch was finally able to calm Stuart down, at least calm him down enough to get the deputy to call the Feds and get an ambulance from Portland. He asked Johnson to stay put at the Billings house and wait for the medics to arrive, and in the meantime, search the area for clues as to who did this. Both men knew who was responsible but neither of them wanted to say the names out loud.

After hanging up the phone, Mitch began pacing around his office. He is lost in thought, trying to wrap his mind around the fact that it couldn't just be a coincidence that these killers were seen in town and now Mr. Billings is found missing his eyes. Stuart said the old man was breathing but was unconscious and unable to speak. It's not likely he will be able to tell the sheriff who did this to him for a while, if he's lucky enough to survive.

Mitch turns and looks out into the station as Sloane begins to walk toward his office. Just the sight of her makes him feel a little more comfortable, as if she will somehow make this whole thing better and has the answers to the dozens of questions he's been asking himself. She swings the door to his office open and gives him a hug. Her arms drop to her side when he doesn't return the embrace and she looks deeply into his eyes.

"Oh my, what's wrong? Are you upset with me about something?" She takes a step away from Mitch, trying to gauge his unhappiness.

"Oh no, it's nothing to do with you. Sit down, we need to go over a few things." Mitch sits behind his desk and begins to tell her what Stuart found, first about the Arroyo brothers and The Butcher and finally about the condition of the senior Mr. Billings.

Sloane is a transplant to town from California, so she doesn't have the same attachment to Mr. Billings as the residents do. She didn't sit in his classroom for an hour a day throughout high school, listening to the man exude his passion for prose and the meaning behind the works of Poe and Shakespeare. She didn't have the chance to listen to his voice or refrain from laughing at his corny dad jokes that would come whenever the opportunity arose. Because of this, she doesn't take the news with the same passion as Mitch had hoped she would.

Most people would have been horrified to find out what happened to Mr. Billings. Sloane, however, is not an ordinary person. She lives for the thrills. Hearing the news has brought her to the edge of her seat, hoping for more excitement and some actual police work, waiting to hear what they are going to do next. She may even have a bit of a smile on her face. There is a long period of silence after Mitch finishes his retelling of what Stuart found at the house.

"Well, what are we going to do Mitch? We can't just sit here and do nothing!"

"I don't know what we can do. We have no idea who is responsible for this."

"The hell we don't. Look, I know you don't want to believe anything that guy told you last night, but it seems to be a little more than a coincidence to me. These Mexican guys work in a different way than you and I are used to. It has to be them."

Mitch rummages through the printed-out articles on his desk, "you may be right, but it's not like they are just going to hang around and wait for us to find them. I bet they are long gone by now."

"Maybe they are or maybe they're not. Jesse said that the mayor was mixed up in something. Maybe these men paid him a visit next." Sloane slumps back in her seat, obviously frustrated at the lack of urgency from the sheriff.

"I guess I could go out and have a talk with the mayor, but I doubt he will be forthcoming with any information."

"Correction. We will go pay him a visit," Sloane demands.

Mitch looks up at her, surprised he didn't see that response coming. "That's not a good idea. What if these guys are there and the situation becomes dangerous?"

Sloane chuckles slightly. "I love that you want to protect me, I really do, but if these guys happen to be there, it's probably you that needs the protection."

Mitch smiles and rolls his eyes. He takes a moment to think about what course of action to take. On one hand, he doesn't want to face these Mexican killers all alone, but on the other hand, if he does face them, he doesn't want Sloane to be anywhere nearby. He has already suffered through the loss of his father and Deputy Carter this season, losing Sloane might be more than he could handle.

"I'll make you a deal. You can ride along with me to the mayor's place but if I see anything that looks odd, you'll stay in the car. Deal?"

"Sure Sheriff. Anything you say."

Mitch has known her long enough now to know when Sloane is not being completely honest with him, but in the end, he would rather have her with him than to face these men alone. A small part of him hopes that when they head to the transportation offices, that it's business as usual. There is a small chance that the attack on the senior Billings could be completely unrelated to the new visitors to town, but it doesn't seem likely.

"I'll call Stuart and let him know we are heading down to have a word with the mayor. You go get changed and let Lucille know what the plan is. Tell her to expect some calls from the Feds regarding Mr. Billings and that she is to tell them that we have everything under control."

Sloane gets up from her seat and turns to exit the room without saying a word. She is almost giddy with excitement and Mitch sees the extra pep in her stride.

"Sloane," she stops with her hand on the knob of the door and turns to face him. "Make sure your gun is loaded."

She smiles at him, "you've known me long enough by now to know that my gun is always loaded."

Chapter 18

Mayor Harry Billings, like most of the other residents of Twisted Timbers, has been here his whole life. He has dealt with the taunts from his classmates because his father was a teacher. He has heard the people make fun of him because of the few extra pounds he has always carried around. He has learned to live with the ribbing and bullying. It has helped mold him into the man he has become. He has learned to be self-dependent and build a good life for himself. Sure, the people in town think of his trucking company as a joke, and the mayor knows that the revenue that shows up on the company's accounting paperwork isn't exactly accurate, but he built this company from the ground up and he's proud of that fact.

Even as a child, Harry Billings was always trying to hustle someone. His family wasn't poor but living on a teacher's salary doesn't allow for some of the nicer things that the other kids in town always had. The problem with growing up with the last name of Billings is that Harry knew if he wanted the nicer things in life, like the other kids his age had, he would have to get them on his own. When he was just a freshman in high school, Harry would sneak into his father's office and steal the answers to the final exam. He would then sell the answers to the test to the senior class, which made him popular with the older kids, which to Harry was the only thing that mattered.

Despite the rumblings from the people in town, he has built this trucking company from nothing. Sure, the land was given to him by his father, but back then it was just an empty patch of dirt. As he sits behind his desk and stares out at his new Lexus, Harry feels accomplished. He feels like a big man when he walks down the streets in town. Sure, the people may laugh when he goes by, but the fact remains that he is a business owner and the mayor. He hasn't really worked hard for what he has, the land for the business had been in the family for generations. His title as mayor was given to him as well, there are no formal elections in such a small town. He leans back in his leather chair and kicks his feet up onto his oversized mahogany desk.

The prospect of bringing a year-round resort to town is going to be his legacy. The one thing in his life that people could not say was given to him. He has worked diligently to work out the details with Cassie Reynolds and the fact that he stands to make a large chunk of cash from the sale of the land where his company now sits, is just icing on the cake. Closing the trucking company will not be that hard and firing the seven employees he has would be strictly business.

He has allowed for his employees to leave work early today, a tradition popular with locals to avoid the onslaught of traffic for the holiday weekend. He enjoys the peace and quiet of the office and warehouse when nobody else is around. It allows him to clear his mind and focus his attention on the obstacles that still face him regarding the proposed land sale, the biggest of which is to have his father officially sign over the deed. Once that issue is resolved, it would only be a matter of days before the seven-figure sum would be in his account and he could finally leave town for good. He closes his eyes and drifts asleep with thoughts of sun, sand, and a place far away. A place where his name and his past doesn't precede him.

He is rustled awake by his feet falling from the desk and his body tumbling out of the rolling chair. He instinctively looks around the room to see if anyone is laughing at him, a habit he learned during his younger years. The sun has begun to set outside, throwing dark shadow into the corners of the room. It's nearly dinner time and the mayor finds a sudden boost of energy along with a hankering for a steak. He grabs the keys to his car from his desk and starts to head for the door when he is face to face with a large man he has never seen before.

"Sit down," the man says as he puts both hands on the mayor's chest.

Harry Billings stumbles backwards, trying to find a way around the large man. The behemoth towers over the mayor and is far wider, but not in the same soft, fleshy manner as Harry. After a few seconds of uncoordinated and clumsy jostling, the mayor collapses in the chair and begins yelling at the man. "Who are you? How did you get in here?"

The man swings his arm out wide and releases a vicious backhand that catches Harry on the cheek, sending strings of spit across the room. "Shut up, you rat."

The mayor is left speechless and holding the side of his face. He has never seen this man, but his size and strength are intimidating to the extent that he doesn't want to move and feel the wrath of the backhand a second time. He just looks up, trying to fight back the watering of the eyes, and stares at the foreign man.

Two more men appear in the doorway, barely visible behind the imposing figure of the first. A smaller, skinnier version of the first guy, walks in and begins to wrap a rope around the mayor. He cinches it tight, with assistance from the big man, and the two of them spin the chair around so the mayor is facing the third man. This guy is tall and slender, every hair on his head is perfectly in place and his clothing looks like what you find in a gangster's handbook, right down to the pin-striped suit. The man has brown skin, faded and tough from years in the hot Mexican sun. He walks slowly across the room, stopping right in front of Harry Billings without looking at him.

The mayor now knows who his visitors are, and the thought causes him to weep softly. He knew there was a chance that he would meet them, but he was hoping to escape town before his shady past would be able to catch up to him. Unfortunately, the presence of these men in his office nails home the fact that this time, he will be unable to hide his wrong doings.

"Do you know who I am?" The leader talks slow and deliberate, with the tone of a person who is speaking a language he knows but is not completely comfortable with.

In response, the mayor simply nods his head.

"Do you know why I am here?"

Again, nothing but a nod from the mayor.

"This should be fairly easy then. Do you have what belongs to me?" The Butcher looks down on the mayor and speaks to him like a father talking to his son who has just got caught stealing a peek at the dirty magazines kept under the bed.

This time the mayor looks straight into the man's eyes and shakes his head slowly in denial.

"Ah, then a problem we have," the man says in his broken English. He is rubbing his hands together and making barely audible noises with his mouth. "Then I wonder what I should do with you. I came a long way to find you, and to get back what is owed to me. How about I start by telling you a story?"

The mayor looks at the man, who is now pacing across the floor in front of him. He strides confidently past him several times, seemingly in no rush or having any anxiety about being here. Harry knew when he got into business with this man that he had a reputation of being ruthless, but Harry also thought it would be some easy cash and would be his nest egg to make his life easier. He made the arrangements long before there was any indication that Cassie Reynolds had any plans to invest in the area.

"There was a young boy in the village where I grew up. One time, he was caught stealing from the garden of a neighbor. This boy was very hungry and just wanted to eat. The man who owned the crops caught him and brought him into the house. He beat the boy, several times." The slow draw from the man makes every word sound differently than an American would say them and adds to the intensity of the situation. "This boy was beaten until he begged the man to stop. The man grabbed the boy by the face and looked him in the eye, before telling him that he is getting beaten because he is not only stealing from the farmer, but he is taking food straight from the mouth of his family." The man stops in front of the mayor and looks down at him. "I have never forgotten this lesson, and I have never forgotten the beating I took that day. I tell you this so that you know why I am going to do to you, what I am going to do. Stealing from me is like taking food from my mouth."

The whimpering mayor is no longer trying to hide his fear. "I didn't steal from you, sir." The usual cocky man has been left pleading for his safety.

"Do you have what belongs to me then? Give me what is mine and we will be out of here."

"I… I don't have it. I mean, there's still some in the trucks, but the rest has been sold." Mayor Billings is usually good at talking his way out of certain situations. This is not one of them.

"Then, mi amigo, I'm afraid it's going to be a very long night for you." The man shoves his hand in his jacket pocket and digs for something inside. He pulls his hand out slowly, causing the mayor to fear he is pulling a gun and he tries to wiggle his face out of range of a weapon. "You think I am going to let you off that easy? Did you listen to the story I told you? I was beaten for several hours for stealing a few potatoes.

You have taken much more than that from me gringo. You will suffer much more. More than your father in fact."

The mayor looks up at the mention of his father. What did his old man have to do with any of this? His relationship with his dad has not been the greatest, especially since his mother passed away, but his father had nothing to do with any of this. "What have you done to my father? He has nothing to do with this."

The man acts as if he hadn't heard the words and bends closer to the mayor. He had removed a cloth from his pocket and now holds it in front of Harry. El Carnicero slowly removes layers of the cloth, revealing the bloody contents to the man in front of him. The gruesome eyes of his father are now staring at Harry, causing the mayor to throw up down the front of his shirt.

The Butcher laughs loudly, folding up the cloth and tucking it back into his pocket. "I talked to your father. My associates thought he was the man that took my money. Unfortunately, your father had to pay a price for your thievery."

The man stops walking and stands in the middle of the room for a brief moment. He begins speaking in Spanish to the two other men, who quickly leave the room. The mayor has no idea what he said to them but whatever it was, it now left him alone in the office with this maniac.

"Mayor Billings. I hope your nap was a good one because you are in for a very long night. When it is all over, you will be dead, and I may even decide to set your entire town on fire."

Chapter 19

It has taken far too long to get going and leave the station. On the phone call to Stuart, Mitch was most worried with the condition of Mr. Billings. Deputy Johnson assured the sheriff that the old man was holding on and is still breathing, even though Stuart was finding it increasingly harder to sit in the same room with the man. The sounds of agony and pain were apparently too much for the deputy to deal with. He assures the sheriff that the medics told him they would be there shortly. Before hanging up the phone, Mitch reminds Stuart that he is not to mention anything about The Butcher or the Arroyo brothers. The last thing Mitch wants to see is a boatload of federal officers flooding the already packed town this weekend.

Sloane saunters back into the office, fully dressed in her uniform, including Kevlar vest. She knocks on the door to Mitch's office and lets herself in. "I'm ready when you are," she proclaims.

Without replying, Mitch gets up from his desk and the two make their way out of the building and into the available patrol car. There is a brief moment of awkwardness as Mitch pauses as he stands outside of the car door, wondering about the protocol regarding opening the passenger door to allow Sloane to get in. If they were not on-duty, he would never let her open the car door for herself. Deputy Nichols must not have felt the same as Mitch, or she wanted to ease the tension for her man, because she just climbs into the car without hesitation.

The two remain quiet as they drive south out of town, until they reach the winding, hilly roads that lead to the Billings property. Sloane breaks the silence first. "Can you give me more background on the mayor? I didn't grow up here and I have no idea about what kind of person he is."

Mitch turns down the radio before answering her question. "First of all, his father is an icon in town. Any kid who went to school here in the last twenty years has had him as a teacher. This had to be hard on Harry. I'm sure kids made fun of him his entire life." He slows the car down enough to safely maneuver the sharp bends in the road. "Harry is a piece of work and somewhat of a joke to the residents. They feel like he has been given everything in life. The land where his company is, the place we are going, has been in the family for generations. He didn't buy it or even earn it. Some people say his father let him use it to get him out of the house and out of his hair. Even his title as mayor was never earned. In case you haven't noticed, we do things a little differently in Twisted Timbers. We have no elections, and quite frankly, I'm not sure anyone else really wanted the job."

"Why would someone not want to be mayor?" Sloane has always lived in the big city, where the title of mayor is prestigious and comes with power and respect.

"People around here want to mind their own business. It's a hard life to live here. You have to make your yearly salary in the span of a few months, and if you don't, your family pays the price all winter. This is stressful and time consuming. People don't want to spend their valuable time dealing with town issues or being the first face tourists see when they come to town." Mitch takes his eyes off the road long enough to give Sloane a tilted look, trying to emphasize his point.

"What about his trucking company? You told me earlier that it's some sort of joke around here. He must have done something right, it's not easy running your own company."

"Like I said, the land it sits on was given to him. It started with just one truck, an old beat up thing. People would hear it coming from miles away, so they knew how often the thing would come and go." Mitch continues to efficiently navigate the road while appearing like he is hardly paying attention to it. "To hear the old guys tell it, the company has never turned a profit in the seven years it's been around. I, on the other hand, would prefer that the company become prosperous enough that Harry Billings no longer has time to be mayor and he can get off of my back for a change."

Sloane grins slightly, knowing how much Mitch detests the man. "So, he takes the position as mayor a few years ago, you saw him driving around in a shiny new car and he dresses like a mafia scumbag. Sounds to me like the man is desperately seeking attention. That, or else he is trying hard to make up for what he lacks in other areas."

"Like personality," Mitch chimes in as he stops the car a few feet away from the gravel driveway for the trucking company. He begins moving forward much slower, trying to pull down the road with as little noise as possible. The overhanging trees cascade over the road from both sides, making it look like a covered bridge. After several turns, the driveway opens up to a large parking lot. Mitch brings the car to an abrupt stop behind a few bushes and smaller trees that work well in hiding the cruiser from anyone inside the warehouse but allows them to see the parking lot clearly. He shuts down the engine and sits staring out the windshield.

"This is not what I expected to see."

"What do you mean Mitch?"

Mitch takes his time, searching for the words to describe what he is seeing. "I was out here a few months ago. None of these trailers were here and there were only two trucks, and they were well past their prime." As he looks out onto the parking lot, Mitch can see at least six brand new trucks and at least twice as many trailers and shipping containers. "This looks like the parking lot of a company that is thriving, not one that is the laughing stock of the town."

"All of these trucks are decorated with streamers. Is it possible that they are here to help out with the parade on Sunday?"

"I guess it's possible, but something just doesn't seem right. The title of mayor doesn't come with a boatload of cash and by all accounts, this company isn't doing great either. Add that to the fact that he has a brand-new expensive car, and something just doesn't add up. Grab your flashlight, I want to go get a look inside a few of those trailers."

Chapter 20

Mayor Billings has been alone in his office for several minutes. He has not seen or heard the other men for quite some time. The room is quiet, causing Harry to become even more afraid of what is going to happen to him. He knew he was getting into business with a very bad man, but he never thought the man would come looking for him so quickly. He wonders what the three Mexican men have in store and has already began trying to spin the situation in his head. He was alone in his office when the men came in and tied him to the chair, which could work in his favor. If he can negotiate a release, no one else in town will even know the men were here. Little does the mayor know the extent of violence El Carnicero is capable of and has shown on multiple occasions in the past.

The mayor struggles against the ropes, straining his rarely used muscles in ways that have little effect on the strong fibers. The fighting and jostling has only managed to increase his heart rate, increase the amount of sweat soiling his clothes and increase the anxiety and fear he is feeling. His mind drifts to what The Butcher showed him, wrapped up in the cloth and covered in blood. The greedy man begins to smile, thinking that the death of his father could prove quite fortuitous and profitable. With the old man out of the picture, he would no doubt be the heir named in his will, thus having sole ownership of the land he is trying to sell. All he needs to do now is talk himself out of these restraints and out of this situation.

The two men who work for The Butcher burst into the room without warning. They take the mayor and roll his chair through the doorway and out into the large warehouse. There isn't much to the building, it's basically just a metal barn. The large expanse seems like overkill considering that it is less than a quarter full. Random tool boxes and work tables can be seen mixed with a few cardboard boxes and empty broken wooden skids. This is not the kind of building one would expect to see being the headquarters of a successful trucking company.

The bumpy ride comes to a stop in the middle of the massive space, inches from the feet of The Butcher. The expression on the crime boss has not changed since the first time the two men met. He is even tempered, placid with his every movement. The mayor is speaking rapidly, trying to talk his way free. Saying whatever comes to mind, with his words falling on deaf ears. The Mexican man doesn't even look at Harry Billings or acknowledge him with a response. Instead, he looks to his thugs and gives them a few orders in Spanish, along with some drastic hand motions. A few seconds later, the ropes that had secured the mayor to his chair are removed.

At first, Harry thinks that his words have hit home, and The Butcher has decided to work out a truce. Harry begins to slow his breathing, calming his nerves and thinking he may escape this building with his life. From the corner of his eye he catches a glimpse of movement and turns his head, just as the fist of Humberto Arroyo makes contact with his jaw. The blow was quick and powerful. Harry does not lose consciousness, but he is startled, and his head is foggy. His vision is blurry, making it difficult to prevent what the large man is trying to do.

The mayor is a big man, not yet obese, but well on his way. The larger of the two Arroyo brothers still has no problem hoisting the mayor over his shoulder and setting him down on the concrete floor. The mayor is still trying to clear his mind, not really feeling the pain in his face. His senses are picking up the cold floor, the bright lights of the warehouse and hearing the voices who are shouting in a language he doesn't understand. Before he can right himself and attempt to stand up, his wrists are grabbed and shackled inside a spider web of chains. His arms are suddenly rising above his head, lifting the weight of his body up off the ground. The strain on his arms makes his muscles burn and his joints ache. He looks up to the ceiling, notices the chain is connected to the hoist used to lift truck motors away from the chassis for repairs.

The chains go all the way to the ceiling, where the pulley is mounted firmly to a large steel beam. Any hope the mayor had that his measurable weight would cause the hoist to collapse, just vanished. His body is lifted until he is only able to keep his toes on the ground. He has to use every bit of his six-foot frame in order to keep some of the weight off of his arms, which are already becoming numb. The Butcher walks slowly over to him, stops inches from his face and looks him in the eye before spitting a wad of saliva into the face of the mayor.

"You decide to steal from me, now you pay the price. My men might not be as smart as they should, but they are pretty good at hurting people. This weekend, we intend to hurt a lot of people." He turns to the Arroyo brothers and speaks more words that the mayor can't understand. "First it was your father, now it is your turn. When you have taken all you can, and we kill you, we will take out our hatred on this fucking town. All because you thought it wise to steal from me."

The mayor can hardly breath. He has nothing to say to the man and can no longer hold back the emotions. He weeps. His head is hung, and his body is limp. Harry feels the punches to his abdomen, but he does not react to them. He watches as The Butcher hits him several more times, surprised that such a frail, skinny man could deliver a blow with such force.

The Arroyo brothers have been several feet away for the last few minutes. The warehouse is not heated and with every minute, the temperature begins to drop. They have brought over a large metal drum and have filled it with old wooden skids. Juan Arroyo pours some diesel fuel into the container and lights the contents on fire. The whoosh can be heard as the fire ignites and soon the orange glow from the flames sets an ominous shadow on the floor.

Mayor Billings is able to open his eyes long enough to watch the three men huddle together and talk quietly. Juan is the first to leave the huddle, making his way to where the mayor is hanging and yanking off the man's clothes. He leaves him with just his underwear, cutting away what he needs to with a large knife. The larger of the brothers pulls a large metal rod from the fire, the tip glowing bright orange. He examines it and walks swiftly towards Harry. The mayor tries to wiggle his body further away from the approaching man, but his limbs won't allow it. Humberto Arroyo has a slight grin on his face as he watches the tip of the metal rod sear the belly of the overweight mayor. The smell of burnt skin is foul and putrid. A person should never smell his own flesh burning. The act lasted less than a second, and the mayor is unable to see the damage that was caused, but he can feel it.

Just when he felt like he was about to pass out, the mayor notices the panic from the three men. They huddle together once more, speaking quickly. The Arroyo brothers remove guns from their waistbands, guns the mayor never knew they had, and race from the warehouse and into the office. The Butcher sits down in the chair that Harry Billings was once tied to, lights up a cigar and simply looks through the doorway at the weeping man. After a few drags, the smoke rising above his head and forming a cloud, he speaks once again.

"Your night might not be as long as we first thought. It looks like you may have someone to keep you company." The man leans back in the chair and chuckles. "As long as my boys don't kill them too quickly."

Chapter 21

Sheriff Thompson and Deputy Nichols walk slowly through the gravel parking lot as they make their way to the closest of the shipping containers. The early evening sky, with the assistance of the surrounding trees, has covered the area in dark shadows. They shine their flashlights in front of them to lead the way, being careful and cautious. They haven't seen anything that has made them be fearful, but Mitch is a firm believer in trusting your gut. From the moment he pulled into the lot, his gut has been telling him that things are not as they should be.

This first trailer, which is sitting far away from the others, is old and rusted. They can tell right away that several of the tires are flat and the entire thing is leaning to the left slightly. They give a quick look inside and find it empty, with the exception of a few leaves and animal feces. Mitch motions with his left hand and points to the trailers that are parked closer to the warehouse building. These trailers are the few that have trucks attached to them.

They make the short walk to inspect the newer trailers. These are not shipping containers but are the normal freight trailers that travel the highways on a regular basis. There are four of these, lined up in two rows, with all four trucks looking to be no older than a few months. When Mitch looks at the shiny equipment, all he can think about is the cost of the machinery. He has no idea how much a new tractor costs but seeing them in this gravel parking lot, outside the simple and cheap-looking warehouse, further sparks Mitch's idea that the mayor is getting financial assistance from another means.

The two officers split up, Sloane Nichols heads off to inspect the two trailers on the left and Mitch takes the ones on the right, the side closer to the building. The first trailer the sheriff looks in is empty, but a foul odor escapes when he opens the large metal door at the back. He can't identify the scent but decides that the lack of anything visual makes it impossible to figure out the source. He turns his attention to the last of the trailers on his side of the lot.

As he opens the door, it lets out a moan, the heavy door straining to swing wide. Mitch shines his flashlight inside and the light catches several crates and boxes. He grabs ahold of the opposite door, which is still closed firmly, and uses it to hoist himself inside. The big wooden crates are lined up on one side of the trailer, most are still sealed tightly. Mitch unsuccessfully tries to pry one open, but only manages to drop his light. As he reaches to pick it up, he notices the light has inadvertently lit up the contents on the opposite side. The cardboard boxes are opened, with packing tape hanging from the loose flaps.

As soon as the sheriff sees what's inside the box, he realizes that this is the source of the mystery smell in the previous trailer. Even though the small bundles are wrapped tightly in plastic, the smell still burns through the nasal passages. A quick count shows that there are over two dozen of these bundles, which Mitch has deduced could only be marijuana. The inexperienced sheriff could not even ponder a guess as to the value of such a large amount of illegal weed, but if all of these trailers were filled with the same thing, it would explain where Mayor Billings is getting the cash for all of the trucks.

"Mitch, you might want to see what I found." Sloane has made her way around to the back of the trailer Mitch is standing in. Her voice is quiet, obviously trying to remain unseen from anyone else who may be on the property.

"You find something bigger than this?" Mitch waves his arm from side to side, showing Sloane what he found inside the box. "I'm dying to find out what's in these crates. I'm not very good with foreign languages, but this sure does look like Russian lettering to me."

"Mitch, I need you to get down and come see what I found." Her voice is stern and serious. A tone that Mitch has rarely heard come out of her mouth.

He climbs down gingerly and follows Sloane to the other side of the lot. She opens the door slowly and stands behind it as it swings open. Mitch steps in front of the opening and before he is even able to shine his flashlight inside, he is once again hit with a strong smell. This is far different from what he smelled in the other trailers. This scent is a mixture of urine, sweat and human feces. He hesitates for a second before shining his light inside, the beams reflecting from several eyes.

The faces staring back at him are numerous and tear-filled.

He looks at Sloane, "what in the hell are they doing in there?"

"Your guess is as good as mine."

"Any idea how many there are?" Mitch tries to count the number of people, but there are so many people packed tightly together that he can't tell where one body ends and another one begins.

"I haven't got a clue. This is how I found them. They must be scared because they haven't even tried to escape."

"I don't like this Sloane. We need to get these people as far away from this lot as we can." Mitch slowly closes the door back, thinking that if they suddenly had dozens of strangers running through the parking lot, everyone in town would know they were here.

"Let me check something." Sloane hurries from behind the trailer and races to the driver's side door of the tractor. She slowly opens the door, looks inside and races back to Mitch. "The keys are inside, just like the one I checked first.

"That's odd, but I'm not sure that helps us out. I have no idea how to drive one of these things."

"Yeah but I do." She smiles at him, a look that tells him that there is far more that he has yet to learn about her.

"I didn't know that. Do I want to know how you know how to drive one of these things?"

"Probably not. The fact is that I learned how a long time ago. I'm sure I remember enough to get this thing far enough away from here that the people inside will be safe."

Mitch looks at the giant truck again, then back to Sloane. "I wish I could let you do that. It's just too risky. Plus, I don't think either one of us should stick around here alone."

"Mitch, I will just drive it a couple of miles down the road, then I'll run back here. I'm the only one that can do it. If you tried, you would keel over and die before ever making it back here."

Normally, this would have drawn a smile from Mitch, but right now he has more important things to think about. Her logic is sound, she would be the best person for the job, but what would it say about him if he let his girlfriend save these people while he stood here and watched her.

Sloane must have noticed the turmoil he was facing and ended it by simply climbing into the rig and fastening the seat belt. "Look, I know you have issues with me doing things because I'm a woman, but this is not the time. You cover me. This thing is going to be loud when I start it up. If someone is here, they will surely hear it and come running."

Mitch nods his head and tells her to be careful before pushing the door closed. He draws his weapon and takes up a position at the opposite side of the truck. A loud grumble breaks the silence as the monstrous engine comes to life. Mitch scans the building and all the exits for a sign of life and finds none. A loud pop and a small jerk from the tractor reveal that she may know what she is doing in the driver's seat but may be a little rusty.

Sloane slowly ushers the tractor trailer around in a large circle, pointing it toward the road where they parked the patrol car earlier. Mitch watches her as she bounces in the seat, the potholes in the parking lot throwing her body around like a ragdoll. He hears the gears grinding, a unique sound of metal on metal, as she starts to pick up speed. She makes the slight left and he watches as the vehicle exits the lot and begins down the road. As the lights disappear behind the trees, Mitch hears the sound of feet on stone. He turns quickly toward the building and feels the force of a hard object making contact with his head, moments before his body hits the ground and everything goes dark.

Chapter 22

Mitch has no way to tell how long he was out on the ground. He is being lifted back to his feet by two men, Juan and Humberto Arroyo. He looks both men in the face and instinctually reaches for his gun, which is nowhere to be found. His legs are wobbly, and he can feel the trickle of blood coming down the side of his face. The two men are almost choreographed in their actions, the larger of the two using his strength to hold Mitch up and the other man applying just enough pressure on the sheriff's back to lead him where they want him to go.

Mitch can't walk, his feet dragging through the rocks as the Arroyo brothers lead him to the warehouse. He knows Sloane will come back for him, but she is expecting him to be waiting for her. He wonders what the strong-willed woman will do when she comes back and he is not there. He has little time to think about this as his cloudy mind is hit with the sound of a large explosion from behind him. The two brothers stop walking long enough to allow Mitch to turn his head.

The ball of flames can be seen high above the trees. The sun has completely set now, making it easier to see the fire. Instantly Mitch knows that this explosion had to come from the truck Sloane was driving, or attempting to. He can't hold back his anger. His body completely gives up and he attempts to drop to the ground, causing Humberto Arroyo to strain to hold him up. His look never leaves the fire, even as he is being dragged closer to the warehouse. He was a fool for letting Sloane drive that truck out of here, and now she is dead. There is no way she could have survived an explosion like that.

Juan Arroyo races forward and swings open the door to the building before his brother gets there. Once inside, they drop the sheriff on the concrete floor where he buries his head in his hands and cries loudly. This is the second deputy that he has lost in his only season as the town sheriff, but this one hurts far worse. This one he loved.

"Stop crying, you big baby."

The voice startles the sheriff. He doesn't want to look up and face the reality of being a prisoner. He assumes the speaker is one of the two men who pulled his lifeless body into this room. He raises his head, ready to fight and argue with the men. In front of him stands a tall, slender man who is far older than the Arroyo boys. He recognizes this man from the newspaper articles he read earlier in the day as El Carnicero, or The Butcher.

Mitch allows his gaze to go past the Mexican killer and focuses on the body hanging from the ceiling. Mayor Billings is sobbing and looks to be in pain. His normally perfectly placed hair is disheveled, a look the sheriff has never seen. There is a large red circle near the belly button of the portly man, but other than that, he seems to still be alive.

"Do you know who I am? In your country they call me The Butcher." He elongates his name, making the two-syllable word sound like it now has at least four.

Mitch nods. "I know who you are. You are the man who just killed a truckload full of innocent people and the only girl I ever loved."

The man laughs. He actually laughs hysterically. Mitch is appalled by this action but can't find the energy to mount an offensive and attack any of these three men. Since seeing the explosion, his body has not functioned properly.

"See the man behind me? He is the reason those people had to die. His greed has brought me here and now the people of this town will pay the price for his crimes. I did not know you would try to drive the truck from the lot, or I wouldn't have wasted our explosives on it." The man circles Mitch as he speaks, looking down on the sheriff as if he is a lower life form. "As far as the girl you loved, there is an expression that you Americans use, there are other fish in the lake. I believe that's right."

Mitch keeps his eyes focused on the feet of the man, and the animal skin boots he is wearing. "Sea. There are other fish in the sea." He has no idea why he decided to correct the man on something as pointless as this. Maybe he just wanted to show the killer that Mitch might be a little smarter than the man bargained for.

"That does not matter. The man hanging over there is in charge of this town. He is your leader. If he commits a crime, the consequences fall on everyone in this hell hole. I have already informed the man that he is in for a long night. My men are very good at what they do. I did not intend for you to be here, but you tried to interrupt our play time. Now, you too, will face the same fate as that man." He points at the nearly naked mayor, his body fighting to keep its balance.

"I have nothing to do with this. I didn't know anything about the drugs, the guns or the illegals that were brought in here on trucks." Mitch is fishing, hoping that the man will confirm his suspicions about the contents of the empty trailers. The man does not oblige.

"You became involved when your girl cop decided to drive away with property that belonged to me. Unfortunately, she got off easy. The people inside that trailer were my property"

"Fuck you!" The words come out of Mitch's mouth without hesitation. What little training he has had would have told him that agitating your captor would not be wise, but the nonchalant way the man talks about blowing up the truck was more than he could take. "You are going to pay for this you low-life goat fucker"

"Ha. Goat fucker huh. I've been called worse by better people than you." This is the last word that the man speaks to Mitch. The Butcher turns his attention to his two thugs and speaks to them in Spanish, so quickly that Mitch thinks it would be hard to understand even if it was his native language.

Mitch stares at him as he makes his way to the office door and out of the warehouse. This man portrays violence and fits the stereotype of a drug lord perfectly. He has no idea what the Arroyo brothers have in store for him but judging by the looks on their faces as they walk closer to him, they are going to enjoy it.

Saturday

Chapter 23

The Butcher has not been seen since Mitch was first taken captive. The Arroyo brothers, however, have been seen far too frequently. Once El Carnicero left the room, Juan and Humberto took Mitch and attached him to the same hoist that holds the mayor. The two prisoners are now back to back, both with hands forced far over their heads. Mitch can keep most of his foot on the floor since he is several inches taller than Harry Billings, but that doesn't make the awkward position any more comfortable.

His ribs are raw from the initial round of body punches that Humberto felt obligated to throw at him, the massive man using his considerable size to create more than enough torque to break a rib or two. Mitch has not been asked any questions, which causes him panic. He would have thought if the purpose of this torture were to extract some information from him, the leader would have come back in and asked him something. Ask him anything. Instead, he is left hanging here with his body pressed against that of the mayor.

When they first tied him up, the Mexicans removed Mitch's shirt. In the beginning, he thought this was just to make the body blows that much more effective. As the time went by, he quickly realized there was another reason. The first time the metal poker had burned his skin, he screamed in agony. It had startled him and woken him up from a pain induced sleep. He could feel the heat burning a small round spot into his chest. He could smell the burning hair as the smoke rose to his nose.

The Arroyos took turns with the metal rod, rising from their chairs around the barrel fire at least once an hour. Juan, the smaller of the brothers, enjoyed the distribution of pain more than his brother. Mitch couldn't see when the men were coming, as the fire is on the side of the room that faces the mayor, but he could tell by the writhing of the man he is tied to, that his turn was coming. Juan Arroyo would hold the heated metal to the skin longer than Humberto. He relished the pain in the men's faces, almost enjoying the screams. Mitch wonders if this is because of his lack of size and strength, making Juan far less intimidating than his oversized brother.

These attacks became more and more frequent as the night went on. The two prisoners were covered in burns, red and instantly blistering. After a particularly intense visit from Juan Arroyo, the sheriff decides he needs to get answers from the mayor. He knows the larger man is conscious after hearing his screams minutes before his own.

"I need to know what's going on. I need to know why these guys are here." Mitch whispers this to the man behind him, trying to turn his head as far as he can.

"It doesn't matter now," say the mayor.

"Look, I am in this as much as you are. If I am going to die tonight, I would at least like to know why."

"You're supposed to be the Sheriff. You're supposed to stop things like this from happening in this town. I knew you were not good enough to do the job. You are nothing like your old man."

The reference to his deceased father infuriates Mitch. "Neither are you. I don't know what you are mixed up in, but it is going to get us both killed."

"I'm still proclaiming my innocence." Says the mayor through heavy breathing.

"I think we are far beyond that stage." One thing that Mitch noticed when reviewing the articles that Stuart printed out was that even though The Butcher is a violent man, he was never accused of harming innocent people. If this trio of bad guys is here and torturing them, then the mayor has had to have given them a reason. "They have seriously injured your father, who I am certain had no idea what you were up to. Now they have me tied up with you. I guarantee you that I had no knowledge of what you were doing. It's time to come clean."

There is a long pause before the mayor replies, "you said they seriously injured my dad. Does that mean he is not dead?" Harry had assumed these men had killed his father after seeing the eyes wrapped up in the handkerchief.

"Stuart found him this afternoon and was in the process of getting him rushed to the hospital in Portland. The last I heard he was still alive." Mitch doesn't relay the seriousness or how gruesome the attack was on his father, hoping to keep Harry Billings focused on answering his questions.

The mayor is silent. Mitch tries to wrench his neck further to make sure he hasn't lost consciousness. He is able to see enough of the room to catch Juan Arroyo getting out of his chair and looking at the two men. Mitch doesn't turn his head away. Instead of going toward the fire to get the metal rod for another round of flesh burning, the small Mexican man makes his way to one of the work benches against the wall. It's easier to see what the man is doing now, as he is directly to the right of the hanging men. Juan tosses several tools aside, obviously looking for something in particular. He finds what he is looking for and holds it up toward the overhead lighting to inspect it. He turns, faces the two prisoners, and begins walking toward them. The look in his eyes has changed. He now looks like he has a new mission, which involves more than simply burning a little skin.

His walk is slow, like a predator who has stumbled on a free meal. He carries a large pair of bolt cutters in his right hand, the metal tool looking like it is much too big for him to wield comfortably. He stops next to the two men and holds the tool close enough to their faces that they have no trouble seeing it. Mitch feels his body strain against the forces of gravity as the mayor tries to nudge his body further away from the Mexican. The uncoordinated movements tighten the chains and cause the mayor to cough loudly before Mitch is able to stop the two men from swaying helplessly.

"We made it clear that there was to be no talking. Now I must punish you."

Mitch watches the man as he uses both hands to lift the set of bolt cutters, the sharp tip just inches from his face. Juan walks away from Mitch, to the mayor's side of the room. The sheriff can't see what is happening, only hearing the once arrogant Harry Billings whimper like a child. Mitch's body is suddenly shaking violently, his ears ringing from the sound of the mayor screaming in protest. Moments later, just as his hearing is coming back, he also hears the unmistakable sound of the sharp edges of the cutters closing quickly. The sheriff has no visual on the activity, but the side of his face feels the warmth from the spray of blood coming from the side of the head of the mayor. Mitch can, however, see the ground where the ear that was recently attached to head of Harry Billings now sits lifeless in a small puddle of blood.

Chapter 24

The spray of blood is warm on the side of the sheriff's face. He feels it drip down and fall from his cheek. He can't seem to look away from the small piece of bloody flesh that sits on the floor. The mayor is now motionless, no longer writhing in pain or swaying from his inability to hold his weight still while hanging from the ceiling. Mitch is oblivious to the fact that Juan Arroyo has lost interest in the mayor and has moved over to his side of the room, still holding the large set of bolt cutters. Mitch can feel the gaze of the man on him, but he refuses to give the Mexican the satisfaction of seeing the fear in his eyes.

"It's your turn, hombre" says the small Hispanic man.

Mitch says nothing in reply, but he does move his head away from the flesh on the ground and toward the voice.

Juan Arroyo stands in front of him and raises the tool toward Mitch's chin. His arms quiver from the size of the instrument, causing the metal tip to bump against the skin several times. Juan's shirt is sprayed with blood. The mayors blood. He slowly moves his hands further apart, causing the sharp ends of the cutters to open slightly. The tip moves around the sheriff's face as Juan tries to figure out how he wants to punish his prisoner and which part of the body he wants to disfigure.

The man is nearly pressed against Mitch as he positions the cutters near the nose of the sheriff. Mitch can smell the scent of cigarettes on his breath and the mustiness of a man who has not showered recently. His added height has allowed Mitch to keep both feet on the floor and with the mayor unconscious, he has no trouble standing in one place with his arms bound overhead. As the sharp edges of the cutters pass by his eyes, Mitch looks past them and right into those of Juan Arroyo, who stands several inches smaller than he does.

Arroyo brings the sharp edges to rest on either side of the nose of Sheriff Thompson and allows the weight of the tool to rest against his face. Mitch can feel the steel press against the soft muscle on his face, just below his eye, but he continues to stare at the man in front of him. He judges how willing this man is to close his hands quickly and bring the sharp edges of the cutters together. Mitch looks for something in the soulless eyes of the man that will tell him if Juan is crazy enough to use this instrument to cut the nose from his face. He gets the indication he needs when Juan winks his right eye at him and his mouth bends in a slight grin.

Mitch decides he needs to act, and act quickly. The man as already done damage to the mayor and the look in his eyes means he has no fear of the consequences of his actions. The sheriff slowly shifts all his weight to his left foot, causing the sharp edge of the cutter to slide a little on his face. He brings his foot swiftly toward the sky and connects with the crotch of Juan Arroyo. The man instantly drops the heavy steel tool and falls to his knees. Within seconds, Humberto Arroyo is at the fallen man's side, having come around the warehouse from an area Mitch couldn't see. He hadn't forgotten about the larger of the two brothers, but while faced with the impending pain from the cutters, Humberto wasn't very high on his priority list.

The two brothers speak a few words in Spanish before Juan is able to right himself and rise to his feet. The smaller man refuses to allow his brother to help him up, using one hand to steady himself and the other to slowly massage the injured area.

"That was not very smart gringo," says Juan with a slightly higher pitch to his voice.

"I have been accused of several things but being smart has never been one of them." Mitch instantly regrets saying this, remembering from the training brochure that he read on hostage negotiations that it's not wise to agitate the suspect.

The humorous reply falls on deaf ears and Juan motions to his brother that he's fine as the larger man returns to the other side of the room, where Mitch can no longer see him. Instead of reaching for the large bolt cutters, Juan digs a knife from his pants pockets and slings open the handle and exposes the blade. In normal circumstances, Mitch would not be intimidated by such a small weapon held by such a small man. Under these circumstances, Mitch is now highly intimidated.

His left foot plods slowly in front of the other as Juan inches his way closer. He stands slightly off to the side, trying to avoid another painful kick from the sheriff. He swings his arm and the blade from side to side, as if he was holding a sword instead of the small pocket knife. Mitch can once again smell the man's breath. He feels the man next to him but can't turn his head far enough to the side to see him.

"You will pay for such a stupid thing. There is nothing you can do now. Nothing except bleed." The words come out slow and deliberate.

Mitch knows he has nothing left to do to protect himself. No other option. He is at the mercy of this man. Right now, he wishes the man held a long sword instead of the smaller knife. A longer blade would make the ending come quicker. This man probably knows how to inflict the most pain to a person with the pocket knife before delivering the final, deadly blow. He has seen the pictures in the newspaper articles, the victims left to die in the streets and alleys of Mexico. As he begins to feel the point of the blade dig into his ribs, he wonders if this man was the person responsible for the slayings or was it his boss.

The knife slides quickly over the skin and Mitch can feel the cut right away. The Mexican didn't use the point of the knife to stab the sheriff, instead he used the razor-sharp edge to slice through the tight skin of his abdomen. The area directly under the wound is warm and moist. The sheriff lets out a loud scream, but quickly gathers his composure. Mitch doesn't want to give the smaller man the benefit of knowing that he has all the power in the situation. Sheriff Thompson takes a few deep breaths, trying to find his happy place, and braces for the next slash.

He can hear the footsteps of the man as he circles behind and then approaches him from the opposite side. The point of the blade returns to the same spot on his abdomen as earlier, just on the opposite side of his body. Mitch encourages himself not to scream this time. He tells himself to be strong, to bite back the pain. The cold blade once again rips through the flesh with ease, but it's not his own voice that he hears echoing through the warehouse.

Chapter 25

The early morning fog is dense and thick, adding to the cloudiness in her mind. Sloane Nichols wakes up with her head pressed against a large rock and surrounded by trees. It's a scary feeling, waking up in a strange place and not knowing how you got there. It's even scarier when you see a pool of blood on the ground near your face. She tries to roll her body over, but between the soreness of her muscles and the fallen branches she is wedged in, the task is harder than it should be. She moves slowly, taking a mental roll call of her body with every movement, until she is able to sit in a prone position.

Sloane looks around, hoping to find some evidence of where she is and how she got here. There is nothing significant when she looks across the valley except for trees and a steep grade, one much higher than the one she sits on now. Behind her is more of the same, although there seems to be a ridge about fifty feet up from her position. It would be a difficult climb, but if it were her only option, she could make it. Sloane has always been confident, even more so when it came to her physical abilities.

She reaches into her pants pocket and pulls out her cell phone, hopeful for a signal. One look at the device and its shattered screen tells her it's useless. Sloane takes a moment to collect her thoughts and figure out a plan. She has no other option than to make the climb up the side of the hill. The footing is treacherous at best, but there appears to be enough fallen trees that will make it easier to use her strength to pull her way up. Every bone aches and every muscle throbs. She has a pounding headache and a small patch of her blonde hair is cemented to the side of her head. She knows that there is no chance of getting out of here if she doesn't make it up the side of the hill and begins the strenuous task.

Sloane has lost all sense of time but is in no hurry to make it to the top. She went on many hikes when she lived in California and was taught at a young age the value of making sure your footing is solid before moving onward. Every step is labored and every muscle screams with pain. A healthy body would struggle to make this climb, but she is forced to do it with an unclear mind and no safety equipment whatsoever. About halfway to the ridge and the clearing, Sloane stops long enough to judge her progress.

The valley below is stunning, now that much of the morning fog has worn away. She looks to her left and is instantly hit with a strong memory. She sees an object further down the hill she is standing on, a large steel vehicle that looks like it tumbled down in much the same way she did. Suddenly, all her memories come back to her in a wave. She remembers going with Mitch to talk to the mayor. She remembers finding the trailer full of people on the lot and volunteering to drive them out of the parking lot to a safer location.

Sounds begin to flood her mind. Sounds she must have heard before ending up here. The grinding of metal as she struggled to find the gears to move the truck. The soft beeping coming from under the passenger seat. Hearing this sound caused her to pull the truck to the side of the road and look under the seat. She had never really seen a bomb before, other than in a movie, but she knew right away what it was.

Without hesitating, she jumped out of the driver's seat and onto the blacktop. Her first instinct was to run away as fast as she could, like any normal person would when they find an explosive device. She had only taken three steps away from the truck when her conscience got the best of her and reminded her of the two-dozen people in the back of the trailer that would have no chance to survive if she left. Sloane quickly returned to the truck, unhooked the airlines that connect to the trailer and pulled the handle that would release the jaws that secure the truck to the bottom of the trailer.

Sloane raced back to the driver's seat and slammed the door. Her mind was racing, knowing that the bomb next to her could blow at any time. She found the lowest gear and released the clutch, causing the truck to jerk forward and jostle her tiny frame against the steering wheel. Once she righted herself, she heard a loud crash and thought her life was over. The truck hadn't blown up and still sputtered ahead at a crawl. A check of the rear-view mirror showed her that she had missed a crucial step in the process of detaching a truck from a trailer.

The large container, full of strangers, shook violently as the front end tilted downward and came to rest on the pavement. Seeing this caused Sloane to cuss out loud, knowing that she failed to lower the landing gear, the feet that come down to make the trailer rest securely on the ground. She watched as the container rocked back and forth, fearful that it would tumble down the side of the steep hill and her attempt to save the people inside would turn into a massacre. She had barely been paying attention to where the truck was heading, choosing to remain focused on the trailer. When the steering wheel violently twisted, making her arms go with it, her head snapped back to the front. She had veered slightly to the right, just enough that the front passenger side tire left the asphalt and pointed the rig down the hill. She fought hard with the wheel, hoping to be able to bring it back to the road, but before she thought to slam on the brakes, the truck had already left the roadway.

The massive steel vehicle began to pick up speed as it plowed its way through the brush and trees, refusing to stop or slow. Once again, sounds are what Sloane remembers most. The snapping of the branches, the crumbling of the steel and the shattering of glass. She knew that if she stayed in the truck, the violent wreck would surely cause the bomb to detonate. She decided that she didn't want to stick around for that. She fought hard to swing open the door as her body was tossed around inside the cab. She managed to kick it open, ready herself and make a leap from the moving truck.

She remembers hitting the ground hard and rolling several times. She remembers her head bouncing off dirt, tree trunks and rocks. It was like her body was a magnet for any hard object, if it was on the hillside, she crashed into it. The tumbling slowed, and she remembers being face down in the dirt. The last thing she remembers is listening to the sound of the truck as it made its way down the hill, waiting for the sound of the explosion. Then it came and she blacked out.

As she looks down the hill at the mangled truck, she realizes how lucky she is to be alive. There are signs of fire or scorching all around the area where the truck came to rest. It must have burned for some time while she was blacked out, and looking at the location of the thing, buried deep in the valley, it's not likely that the blast would have been seen or heard from anyone in town, meaning rescue is probably not coming. She's relieved that she has gotten her memory back but is hit with a whole new series of concerns. What happened to the people in the trailer? More importantly, what happened to Mitch? She remembers seeing him as she drove out of the parking lot of the trucking company. If he had heard the crash or the explosion, he would have come to find her. Why didn't he come to find her?

She struggles back to her feet, desperate to make it to the ridge, which she is convinced is the road that leads to the mayor's property. Her motivation to find out the status of the prisoners in the trailer and the whereabouts of Mitch force her body to neglect the pain. With a final pull and a primeval roar, she rolls her body onto the road and lays on her back to catch her breath. She had hoped to see squad cars lining the street. Instead, all she sees when she opens her eyes is the trailer, which is teetering forward like a toppled monster or a fallen tree.

Sloane walks slowly toward the rear of the trailer. Both doors are still closed, which is the only indication she needs to assume the prisoners are still trapped inside. She opens the door, fearful she is going to regret looking inside. The faces look out at her, perplexed at first, and then scared. She guesses these people have been through far worse in their life to perish from a little tumble inside a metal box. Her mind is still foggy from the trip down the hill, so she can't remember any of the little bit of Spanish she knows. She manages to wave her arm in a motion that tells the nameless faces to get out of the trailer. They slowly begin making their way out. Men, women and children climb down one at a time. She notices a few lifeless bodies remain inside the trailer after the prisoners finish filing out. There is nothing she can do about the ones who are already dead, so she focuses her attention on saving the ones who are still alive. They look at Sloane as if she is both a savior and someone to fear. They do not speak.

She points down the road, the direction towards town, and tells them to run. She says it in English, which garners no response from the prisoners. She is at a lost for what to do. She shouts out the first words that she can think of that they may understand, "muy rapido"! She repeats the words over and over, pointing down the road at the same time. Finally, the group begins to move along the asphalt, like a herd of cattle being led to freedom.

Deputy Nichols leans against the metal frame of the trailer and watches them as they walk away slowly. Her eyes met those of a small child who is being held in his mother's arms. The boy is not crying, but his face is covered in fear. She keeps the stare with the boy until his mother follows the road around a bend and the entire group is out of sight. She feels her heart rate begin to slow to a more normal pace, something it hasn't done since she woke up on the hillside. She gives one last look inside the trailer and says a small prayer for the four or five, she can't tell exactly, who didn't survive the journey. Cautiously, she turns and begins her own slow walk. Her walk will take her in the opposite direction as the prisoners, to the parking lot where she last saw Mitch.

Kevin M. Moehring

Chapter 26

"Stop! I am the Butcher!" The voice bellows loudly as it echoes through the large emptiness of the warehouse. The smaller of the two thugs, Juan Arroyo, stops immediately when hearing the voice of his boss, his eyes never leaving those of Mitch. He slowly lowers the bloody knife away from the face of the sheriff and returns it to his pocket. The Mexican continues to hold the stare, looking at Mitch with the disdain of a man that has unfinished business.

"I am in charge of the situation and I am the one who does the cutting around here. Make yourself useful and go outside and check the lot. Take that fire barrel with you, the smell is making me sick."

Mitch can't see the boss, but his words give him a reprieve, at least for the moment. He is still chained to the overhead hoist, with the lifeless body of Mayor Billings lying restlessly against his own. He hadn't known the time of day, but as Juan Arroyo obediently heads outside, the light of the morning sun shines through the open doorway. He had blacked out several times while El Carnicero was gone, but hearing the sound of the old man's voice has given Mitch a new second wind.

The Butcher talks in Spanish to the second of the Arroyo brothers, Humberto. Mitch feels his grasp on the ground fade as his body begins swinging through the air. He is helpless to stop the swinging and spinning. The force turns his body to face the other side of the room, where he can now see the face of The Butcher and his thug who has unhooked the mayor from the shackles and is carrying him effortlessly across the room. The large Mexican drops the mayor's body onto a work table in the corner of the room. The large back of Humberto makes it difficult for Mitch to see what is happening in that side of the room so he turns his attention back to El Carnicero.

Their eyes meet, neither man ready to concede and be the first to look away. Mitch struggles to match the intensity of the killer, his eyes never seeing near the violence of those of the crime boss. The Butcher continues to stare into his eyes as he speaks more foreign words to Humberto. Again, Mitch has no idea what is being said or what order is being given. He loses his concentration and gives up the lame attempt at a staring contest when the blood curdling scream comes from the corner.

Humberto has turned away from the table and is walking toward Mitch. As his body sways from side to side, he can now see the Mayor has regained consciousness and is whimpering softly. His body is hanging off the metal table like a child in a chair that's too big. His right leg is suspended in an awkward angle, a result of his knee being pinned into the metal vice that has been mounted to the edge of the work space. Even with the poor lighting, Mitch can see the discoloration in the man's knee. Humberto reaches over Mitch's head and releases the chains and allows the sheriff's body to fall over his shoulder. As he is carried through the room toward the office, Mitch can see The Butcher turn the gears that tighten the vice even further, increasing the pressure the metal is putting on the bones of the mayor's knee. The mayor is still screaming loudly when Humberto drops Mitch into a metal chair in the office and leaves the room, slamming the door behind him.

Mitch is relieved to be down from the overhead hoist, even though his hands are still bound together.

He rubs them across his face and high above his head, trying to get the blood flow to return to normal. He looks around the mayor's office, decorated just as he would have guessed it would be. Posters of partially clad women leaning in uncomfortable poses on the hoods of cars are plastered on almost every open space. The mismatched furniture looks like something you would see in a poor kid's dorm room. A large wooden desk sits in the center of the room, a few feet in front of Mitch. Behind that, there sits a metal filing cabinet, the doors dented and beginning to rust. Plastic milk crates are screwed into the walls on either side and holds stacks of magazines, which Mitch could only assume contain more pictures of half-naked women like the ones on the walls.

The screaming from outside of the office has stopped, which could be a good thing or a bad thing. Mitch tries to listen more closely, but quite frankly, he doesn't really care what happens to the mayor from this point. The greed of the man has already caused pain to the elder Mr. Billings, probably killed Sloane and is the reason Mitch finds himself handcuffed in this office. He tries to convince himself that he doesn't care if the mayor is tortured to the point that he begs the Mexicans to kill him. He was raised differently than that though, and he knows that he will do whatever he can to save the mayor, even if the man is responsible for everything.

The door to the office opens slowly and The Butcher strolls in confidently. He sits down and throws his legs on top of the desk, without saying a word. This period of silence goes on indefinitely, much longer than Mitch feels comfortable with. The men continue to stare at each other. Mitch doubts the experienced killer is sizing him up, but the sheriff is indeed looking the man over. There is no sign of weakness in the man's face. He has obviously stared down much more dangerous men in his life than a small-town sheriff.

El Carnicero is the first to break the stare down, but not by speaking. Instead, he takes his legs down from on top of the desk and reaches underneath the large wood shelving. He struggles slightly as he brings up a large contraption covered in wires and metal parts, with several of the wires leading into a cluster of batteries near the bottom. He sets the object on top of the desk and leans back in the chair, peering at Mitch from over the thing.

"What's that supposed to be?" These are the first words Mitch has spoken in a while and come out much more gruffly than his normal speaking voice.

The man across the desk responds with a chuckle. "I forgot how small time you are. This is what you call a bomb. This is one of the things you've seen in movies that go boom. This is how I am going to make this town pay." He speaks to the sheriff in a patronizing manner, as if he explaining something to a small child.

Mitch's first reaction was to shudder when he hears the word. Looking at the object in front of him doesn't make him feel any better. "Doesn't that seem like a bit of overkill? You have an issue with one man, and you are going to take it out on the whole town?"

The Butcher shakes his head softly, "do you not remember the story I told you about stealing the potato?" Mitch doesn't remember any story about stolen potatoes but allows the man to go on, fearing an interruption would only anger him further. "Do you think I would think twice about stealing if the farmer would have given me a light punishment? No. I would have stolen again and again. He beat me to the point where I was hoping to die. He knew doing that would make sure that I would never steal again." His voice has gotten louder and louder, speaking of the pain he suffered as a child obviously striking a nerve with him. "This town decided to make the man in that room their leader. They chose to make him the face of the town. They chose to follow a man who only cared about himself. Now the whole town will pay for their stupidity and his idiotic mentality."

"If you ask me, you're batshit crazy. I say you kill the mayor and go home to Mexico. I hear your favorite goat is lonely." He hadn't known the large man was behind him, but the solid slap to the back of his head let Mitch know that he was no longer alone with the boss.

"I like you sheriff, I really do. I don't like you enough to keep you alive, but I still like you. This town on the other hand, I don't like it. Too many trees. Too many tourists."

"I may be just a small-town sheriff, but I'm smart enough to know that a single bomb won't do much to destroy the town."

"Ha. This bomb will not destroy the town, but when we have a couple of them mounted to the trucks that will be used during the parade, they will give us the result we want." He sits down in the chair once more, apparently pleased to give Mitch the full picture. He rubs his hand along the smooth metal top of the bomb, "this one has a different purpose. It will only destroy this building and the people who are unfortunate enough to still be stuck inside of it. That is, if I can stop my boys from killing you before then"

Mitch takes a moment to ponder the implications of multiple of these explosive devices being detonated somewhere along the parade route. Thousands of people, both residents and tourists, will be lining Main Street Sunday morning and will be oblivious to the impending danger. The Butcher waits expectantly for a response from Mitch.

"You will never get away with it. I have more men and they will be here at any time." This is a bluff of course, but Mitch doesn't know what other choice he has but to try and convince the foreigner that the town has a substantial police presence.

More laughter from the Mexican. "You mean Stuart Johnson? I've seen this guy on the internet. He would probably wet his pants before causing me any issues. I surely hope you are not pinning your hopes on Deputy Johnson."

Chapter 27

The alarm goes off, filling the quiet room with the familiar whistle from the theme song of the Andy Griffith Show. Stuart Johnson reluctantly wakes up and shuts off the annoying sound. He has learned to embrace the fact that the residents think he resembles the lovable Barney Fife and don't really take his title of deputy very seriously. He can smell the breakfast cooking in the kitchen, and it causes him to remember he didn't eat much last night. It's on mornings like this one that he is thankful to still live with his mother, another aspect of his life that causes him ridicule.

Stuart tosses back the blankets and climbs out of bed. He straightens out his two-piece flannel pajamas, decorated with numerous G. I. Joe figures, on his way to the kitchen. He sits at the table and his mother greets him with a plate of bacon and eggs. The food is just what the deputy needs to help wake himself up. Rarely does he come home as late as he did last night, but the surgeries for Mr. Billings took longer than expected. By the time he made the drive back from Portland, it was well after midnight.

For the past few years, his mother has been telling him that being a cop was not good for him. She was convinced that bad things were going to happen to him because of his occupation. It wasn't until the events earlier in the year that he has started believing her. She leaves the room now, obviously feeling the tension in the air. She no longer asks him what he is working on with his job, not wanting to know the dangers that he is putting himself in.

Stuart takes his time eating his breakfast, spending extra time to rehash the events of last night in his mind. He stayed at the hospital until he got the word that Mr. Billings would live, despite losing both of his eyes. He had notified the F.B.I. of the circumstances of the attack and assisted them in scouring the property for any sign that the eyes were on the premises, in hopes that the doctors could work a miracle. They were supposed to be sending special agents and forensics techs down this afternoon to do more inquiries and process the crime scene. Mitch has urged him to keep the situation quiet, but that was not in the realm of possibility. When you show up at the hospital with a patient that had been attacked as brutally as Mr. Billings had, word gets around.

He had tried to call Mitch several times on the drive home and was unable to reach him. He even tried calling Sloane's phone but again had no success. Stuart had begun to worry about the two of them, knowing they were heading to the mayor's property. His worries were put to ease when he drove past Mitch's apartment on his way home and saw both the sheriff's truck and Sloane's little Volkswagen in the parking lot of their complex.

Stuart finishes eating and places his plate in the sink. He tries the sheriff's phone one last time, still no answer, before getting a shower and dressing in his uniform. There was a time he would feel proud to look at himself in the mirror in his uniform. This past year, and the things that have happened in town in that time, has made him think differently about what he wants to do with his life moving forward.

Since he got back to town so late, he brought the patrol car home with him. Before pulling out of the driveway, he tries to reach Mitch or Sloane on the radio but again gets no response. He puts the car in gear and starts the short drive to the station. He can already see the influx of people in town. The line is much longer than normal at the coffee shop, and he decides he will have to bypass his normal caffeine fix. He parks the car in the lot and walks in to the station. He is met with the smiling face of Lucille Pennington. She is always the first person in the building on the weekends and he is relieved to see her working as if it is just another day.

"Good morning Stuart." Her voice is calm and unfaltering. Her face is the same shade of grandmother gray as it would be any other day.

"Hi Lucille. Have you heard from Mitch?"

"Not yet. He should be coming in soon though. It's going to be a busy weekend."

"Yes, it is." He tries to keep his tone flat, not letting on that his gut is telling him something is not right. Mitch is young and has very little experience as Sheriff but it's not like him to be MIA for so long. "I think I'm going to go check things out by the mayor's property. I haven't heard from the sheriff since yesterday afternoon and that was the last place that I know he was going."

Lucille looks up with a small change in her demeanor, a little more concern. "Is something wrong?"

"I wouldn't say that. It's just not like him to not answer his phone." He knows how sensitive the older woman is when she hears about violence in town and decides to not mention what happened to Mr. Billings. "I'm sure he and Sloane just had a little extra to drink and are sleeping it off. It's been a long season this year."

"It feels like this season was never going to end. I can't wait until tomorrow. I have my lawn chair all set up on the curb out front for the parade."

Stuart had been so caught up in the happenings last night, and now this morning without being able to get ahold of Mitch, that he has almost forgotten that this is Labor Day weekend and the parade tomorrow will mark the end of the season. During the long drive home from Portland last night he had come to a conclusion regarding his future. Once the parade was over and things slowed down, he would let Mitch know that he would be resigning his position. He used to love doing his job, back before he was attacked by assassins at Graham Park and nearly skewered in the woods. He doesn't know what he will do for work, but that is a decision for a later time. Right now, all he wants to do is find Mitch and get through this weekend. He makes his way out of the front door, slides back into his patrol car and turns it down Main Street in the direction of Billings Trucking.

Chapter 28

The longer she walks, the more her muscles begin to feel like normal. At first, her pace was slow and deliberate. Her knees creaked like an unoiled door and her head throbbed like a steel drum. The morning air has worked wonders to loosen her joints and clear her mind of the cobwebs. Sloane walks near the trees on the opposite side of the street as the steep drop where the truck went off the road. She doesn't really know how far she was able to move the truck before she saw the flashing lights of the explosive device, but it couldn't have been too far. She remembers the sound of the gears grinding and cussing at herself because she looked foolish in front of Mitch.

The thought of Mitch forces new worries and concerns to creep into her mind. Why had he not come looking for her? Did he run into problems when he confronted the mayor? He surely would have heard the crash or the explosion. As she ponders this, the rear of the police cruiser sneaks into her sightline. Mitch parked the car well off the shoulder of the road, hidden among the overgrown trees and bushes, before entering the parking lot of the trucking facility. She speeds up her pace, crouching slightly as she sneaks up to it from behind.

The fact that the patrol car is still parked where they left it the day before is not a good sign regarding the fate of her man. He has to be on the premises somewhere and is probably in trouble. She works her way around to the passenger side of the car, the side furthest away from the road, using the car as cover in an attempt to stay hidden. She slides into the seat quickly and reaches for the radio. It takes her a minute before she realizes that the lights on the control unit are not lit up like they should be. She turns the small computer, which sits on a bracket mounted in between the front seats, to face her, and sees that it too has no power. She slams down the microphone to the radio in disgust.

When the cord to the microphone expands and retracts, the metal object bounces off of the keys which are still left in the ignition. Sloane grasps for them, hopeful the car will start and recharge the electronics. Unfortunately, Mitch had left the key in the on position. The car had not been left running, but Mitch had used an old cop trick, leaving the keys in the on position in case there is a need to start the car quickly in pursuit of a suspect. The downfall to this tactic, which Sloane is facing right now, is that the amount of electronics utilized in a squad car put an enormous amount of strain on the car's battery. After a few hours, the battery is drained, leaving the radio, computer and any other electronics, useless.

Now that there is no chance that she can call for help or drive back to the station, Sloane begins to seek other options. She hadn't checked for it when she first climbed to the top of the ridge, but her police issued gun is not on her hip where it should be. She's not surprised. She was lucky to survive the tumble out of the truck, a fall that could have easily killed her. A thought crosses into her mind and she grabs the keys and yanks them from the ignition.

Once the benefits from the Graham Park case began to come in, increasing the police budget generously, Mitch decided to equip each of the police cars with a shotgun. Sloane loved the added force of the weapon, having spent several days in Portland training with the new equipment. She opens the trunk and finds it just where it should be. After a quick check to make sure it's loaded and ready to go, she strolls a little more confidently to the parking lot of the trucking company.

She takes her time, weaving in between trailers and large trucks, making sure to point the shotgun in front of her and keeping the barrel pointed in whatever direction she is looking. As softly as she is trying to place her feet, it is nearly impossible to stop the cracking that her boots make as they contact the gravel. She fears for the worse around every corner, not knowing what to expect, but always prepared for it.

Sloane takes up a position behind the last trailer, keeping her eye on the front door to the building. She's smart enough to know that it wouldn't be prudent to walk right up to the door and burst in, even with a shotgun. Instead, she scans the perimeter looking for a second entrance or at least a spot where she can get a look inside without being seen. She has no idea what kind of trouble is waiting inside the building, so any intel she can gather before going in would be in her favor.

The metal siding on the sides of the building seem to be old and not very sturdy. It is possible that two sheets of the thin metal could be separated enough to allow her to see in. The thought of being that close to the building is slightly intimidating to her. She likes to play the tough girl role, but it's much easier to do that when there is at least one other person around. Being alone in this scenario puts her a little out of her comfort zone.

She crouches low and makes a sprint for the left side of the building. She manages to stop her momentum before crashing into the metal siding and letting anyone in the vicinity know that she's on the property. The sound of the gravel flying as she ran was loud enough, but a loud crash into the wall would have been disastrous.

She runs her hands along the metal wall, looking for even the slightest of opening that will allow her to peer in. She walks the entire left side of the building and has yet to find what she is looking for. She turns the corner to the back of the building, the shotgun leading the way, and finds the ground has turned from loud gravel to much quieter dirt and beaten down weeds. She feels comfortable enough to place her ear against the metal, hoping to get a hint as to what is happening on the inside. She hears nothing.

Sloane walks a few more paces and finally finds what she has been looking for. The middle of one of the large sheets of metal is bent outward, like someone had lost their temper and kicked at it several times from the inside. It takes a few seconds for her eyes to adjust to the change in light as she looks through the opening, but there is no sign of Mitch on the inside. She does see the mostly naked body of the mayor laying on a work table in the corner of the room and at first it looks to her like he is dead. She stares at him for a while before she is able to notice that his round stomach is moving up and down slightly.

She tilts her head from side to side several times, trying to get into position to see as much of the room as she can. She is relieved that other than Mayor Billings, there doesn't seem to be anyone else in the building. This is somewhat puzzling to the female deputy. Mitch has to be here somewhere. Is he hiding like she is or is he in trouble and she just can't see him from her location? She leans the shotgun against the metal wall, which allows her to crouch down even lower for a different vantage point. She barely gets her face back to the opening when she feels the breeze from behind and sees the shotgun disappear from her side. She reaches for it and rolls to follow its path as it eludes her.

Sloane hadn't seen the faces of the Mexican hitmen in the newspaper clippings that Mitch studied before they came out here, she had been too busy getting into uniform and trying to convince the sheriff to let her come along. She is seeing the face of Juan Arroyo for the first time as he throws her shotgun far into the woods behind the building and wrapping his hands around her hair, pulling her up to her feet.

"Let me go you piece of shit!" Sloane is trying to kick at the man, but her head is being wrenched in a direction she doesn't want it to go.

"No puta. It's time for you to come join our little fiesta."

Chapter 29

The drive to the Billings Transportation property takes about fifteen minutes. Stuart Johnson is overly cautious as he always is on the curving roads that lead out of town to the south. He does a radio check multiple times along the route and repeatedly fails to get a response from Mitch or Sloane. Their personal vehicles were both in the same spots they were in last night, but he did notice that the other squad car was not parked at the station. It is possible that the they could be having an issue with the radio in the car and that they are in one of the numerous dead zones for cell phone activity in the area. While this is always a possibility, Stuart has the same gut feeling he had when he first walked into the amusement park a few months back. The feeling that today was going to be another day he wished he would have listened to his mother and chosen a much safer profession. He hopes, for once, that his instincts are wrong.

The thickness of the forest picks up as he makes his way out of town. He is running through the possibilities in his head, making a note to check the drop-off on the side of the road in case Mitch and Sloane had an accident and ended up driving their car off the road. This too could explain why neither of them have answered his calls, but again, it's not very likely. He's driven with Mitch enough to know that the sheriff is proficient enough behind the wheel to handle the sharp curves like a race car driver.

He tries one last time to reach them via the radio and gets frustrated before returning the microphone to its holster. He fiddles with it a moment too long and when he returns his eyes to the road, there are several people standing in the middle of the pavement. He slams on the brakes and stops inches from the bewildered face of a mother holding her baby son. He gets out and looks at the faces of the dozen or so bodies walking past him. These people look like they are escaping a war zone. Clothes are barely hanging on their frail bodies. Most of them are barefoot and limping badly. Others are noticeably sobbing while they struggle to put one foot in front of the other, leaning against the person next to them who is in a similar state of desperation.

Despite the condition of these strangers, none of them stop and ask him for help. They look at him with disdain and fail to answer any of his questions. They walk past him like he is not even there, heading around the patrol car and continuing on into town. He turns and watches as the last person goes by, wondering why these people are walking down the middle of the road on a Saturday morning, not a single one looking back to him. He decides they are a problem that will have to be dealt with at another time. He has more pressing issues at hand.

He gets back in the car and continues the drive to the mayor's property. About a half of a mile further down the road, he slams on the brakes once more. On the side of the road, like a large oak tree that had tipped over in a storm, a semi-trailer is leaning on its nose on the shoulder. He quickly runs to the back, opens the door and is hit with the overpowering body odor and stench the escapes. He notices the motionless bodies that remain inside, causing his throat muscles to tighten and his eyes to begin to tear up. Stuart Johnson is far from an elite detective, but even he can deduce that the strangers he saw walking down the road must have come from inside. There is no mistaking the smell of body odor and human feces, along with the similarities in the condition of the walkers and the bodies he is now looking at.

Now the senior deputy knows that something isn't right. He jumps back into his car, failing to see the disruption in the vegetation along the side of the road and the wrecked truck fifty feet below. His heart has begun to pick up speed as he pulls up behind the second squad car, parked near the edge of the gravel parking lot. At first, he is hopeful that this will be a sign that things are normal and he is just overthinking the situation. He quickly realizes that idea was nothing more than wishful thinking.

He looks inside the second patrol car and quickly notices that the radio isn't functioning, which is a good reason why the sheriff was unable to answer him, and turns his attention to the parking lot. He doesn't like to draw his weapon, something he never had to do before this year, but he also likes to be ready for the possibility that he may need it. He runs to hide behind the nearest of the trailers in the lot, looking foolish as he hurries along on his tip-toes, as if that will make the sound of the gravel beneath his feet any quieter.

His body slams into the side of the metal trailer, causing an echoing thud as his shoulder bounces off so hard that he nearly dropped his weapon. He walks slowly along the side of the trailer until he makes his way to the end, the side nearest the building. He takes a moment to catch his breath and try to come up with a plan of attack. He laughs to himself softly when he thinks about coming up with a plan of attack. Stuart is a lot of things, but a person who is capable of an attack is not one of them.

He knows that if there is some kind of trouble, or if the sheriff and Sloane are being held by somebody, he is outmatched and would not be much help to either of them. But in order to find out what's going on, he has to have a look around. He convinces himself that he should be able to sneak around the property, using the trailers and trucks as cover, to investigate enough to give him a sense of what he's up against. After giving himself a pep talk, which consists of reciting the five foot nothing, a hundred and nothing speech from his favorite football movie, he grips his pistol tightly and sticks his head out from behind the trailer.

He makes it safely to the comfort of the next trailer, this time managing to prevent his lanky body from crashing against the side. Like previously, he walks slowly down the side of the trailer, inching closer to the building. Another peek around the edge and he starts to move toward his final spot of cover. After two steps on the gravel, he hears the high pitch sound of a woman's scream. He quickly retreats and plasters his back to the side of the trailer. It's hard for him to know for certain if the voice he heard was that of Deputy Nichols. There was so much panic and fear in the scream that it was hard to tell.

Once again, Stuart is forced to give himself a pep talk, this time just to gain enough courage to stick his head around the corner of the trailer. As he does, he sees his worst fear coming true. He can make out Juan Arroyo walking along the side of the building, dragging Sloane behind him, ushering her to the front door of the building by using a handful of her long blonde hair. The Arroyo brothers are definitely in town and are no doubt responsible for what happened to the mayor's father.

"Nope, nope, nope," Stuart mumbles to himself. This can't be happening in this town. Not again. He remains frozen against the side of the trailer, thankful that his mouth didn't let out a scream that would express how scared he was at the sight of Juan Arroyo. He knew when he pulled his weapon that if he found anything unexpected here, he would be outmatched. Now he knows he is. He has to think. He has to come up with a plan. If Sloane is here, then that also means that Mitch is here somewhere too. He has to be on the inside of the building, and Sloane was trying to rescue him. There is no way the sheriff would allow her to come out here by herself.

Stuart is smart enough to know that he would put up little resistance for two Mexican killers. He doesn't want to leave Sloane inside, where these men will do to her whatever they want, but he needs to go and find help. Protocol would suggest his first call would be to the Feds in Portland. They are supposed to be coming to town later this afternoon to investigate the attack on Mr. Billings, but there is no way they will be able to get here fast enough to help Sloane and they will probably only send a few crime scene technicians and no real field agents. Then the thought pops into his head, practically out of nowhere. There is one person he knows that is already in town and would know what to do. Now Stuart just needs to figure out where he can find Jesse Meyers.

Chapter 30

Mitch hadn't noticed that El Carnicero had left the room. His stare was focused on the bomb sitting in front of him. The large metallic instrument looked seriously deadly. Mitch is like most people, when you hear the word 'bomb' you get images of long cylinders that are dropped from fighter jets or giant box-shaped devices that have a timer counting down. The one in front of him looks like neither but it has kept his attention for the last few minutes.

It isn't until he feels the hands of the larger Mexican man scoop him up off the chair that Mitch notices the sounds from the other room. The screams are horrifying. High-pitched and ear-piercing, the noise echoes through the open doorway that leads into the main warehouse. Humberto Arroyo is carrying Mitch over his shoulder, like a sack of potatoes, and drops him on the floor in the middle of the large, open area.

The sheriff can roll his body just enough to see that The Butcher has decided that the knee of the mayor has taken enough abuse and has begun a different kind of torture. The right hand of Mayor Billings is now secured in the same metal vice as his knee was, with fingers bent in a fist. El Carnicero turns the metal rod that tightens the vice slowly and Mitch can hear the tiny bones snap, crackle and pop louder than his morning cereal. The mayor no longer screams. He has been defeated. The evil Mexican man looks back at the sheriff on the floor and spreads his lips in a smile only far enough to show off the gold capped tooth in his mouth.

All heads in the room turn, except that of the passed-out mayor, at the sound of the large metal door to the outside opening and bringing with it a full beam of early afternoon sunlight. Mitch feels his breath stop and his heart accelerate. He begins to crawl to the people that enter the room, only to be stomped in the lower back by Humberto and forced to stay put. The smaller of the two Mexican thugs proudly strolls into the warehouse with a smile from ear to ear. Sloane Nichols stumbles through the door with far less pride, being drug by the handful of her blonde hair which is twisted around the fingers of the little man.

"Boss. Look what I found!" exclaims Juan Arroyo as he shoves Sloane into the middle of the room. "Apparently the bitch isn't dead!"

The Butcher looks at the man, then at Sloane, then back at his man. His face shows pleasure at the find as he saunters over to the female deputy. He walks around her slowly, causing the blood in Sheriff Thompson to boil. There is nothing he can do to stop whatever is going to happen. Humberto hovers over him like an over-sized watch dog that's ready to attack. The Butcher is sizing up the woman. He stops for a moment behind her and runs her hair through his slender fingers, bending in slightly to smell her aroma.

"Leave her alone you piece of shit!" This outburst lands another kick from the watch dog and forces Mitch's body back to the concrete.

"This little lady is most elusive. I thought she was dead, as did you. It changes nothing of course; our plan is still the same, now it will just be more fun for me." The tall man looks at Mitch while resting his head on the should of Sloane and running the blade of his pocket knife across her chest.

"If you touch her, I will kill you." He struggles to get the words out and braces for another assault from above. The kick is delivered as anticipated.

"Ha." The killer lets out a genuine laugh. "You have heard of my reputation. Do you think I have gotten to where I am in this world by not being able to handle people like you? I have fought men twice as tough as you over the years, simply for pleasure. You Americans all think you are tougher than you really are. You've watched too many movies. Or maybe, just maybe, you are still holding out hope to be rescued by the almighty Stuart Johnson. The deputy that even the town folk refer to as Deputy Doofus."

Mitch has nothing to say to this. Stuart doesn't necessarily strike fear into people. There is no way that he would be a match for these three, this trio of men who kill people for pleasure. These foreigners who have made their reputation on slaughtering dangerous men. On most days, the most dangerous thing that Stuart does is play Scrabble with his mother.

Sheriff Thompson feels helpless. He tries to figure out how his father would handle a situation like this, but he has a hard time. He knows his father would have never allowed the situation to get to this point. His dad always knew what was happening in town and had a much better finger on the pulse of the community than Mitch does. The sheriff is young and hasn't mastered the fine art of being the man in charge yet.

Sloane looks at him. Her eyes show the fear and helplessness the woman is feeling. He has never seen this expression from her in the past. She is usually raring to go and always up for a challenge. She too sees the dire predicament they have found themselves in. Mitch knows that Sloane has one giant thing that she must worry about that he doesn't. She is a good-looking woman. In Mitch's eyes, she's the best-looking woman he has ever seen. With her being captured, there is no telling what The Butcher will do to her. Mitch doesn't want to think about it. He eyes the trio of men as they speak Spanish amongst themselves. He can't hear what is being said, not that he would understand any of it even if he could.

The huddle breaks up and the smaller of the two men brings over two chairs and sets them up in the center of the room, side by side. The Butcher returns to the office and closes the door as the larger Mexican, the watchdog, scoops Mitch up from the floor and again tosses him over his shoulder. He drops him like a ragdoll into one of the waiting chairs as the smaller man drags Sloane into the other. The two deputies are tied together, with backs touching, while facing in opposite directions. Sloane is facing the front door of the warehouse while Mitch is forced to look at the motionless body of Mayor Billings. Neither one of them knows what will happen next, but they both know that Stuart Johnson, and his lack of courage, is the only hope they have left for rescue.

Chapter 31

Stuart Johnson races back to town. The fallen trailer goes by in a blur and he doesn't even give a second look as he passes the line of strange looking people walking barefoot. Something odd is going on at the transportation warehouse and somehow Mitch and Sloane are involved. He is the only deputy left, but he is also aware of his limitations. He didn't grow up watching cop shows and hoping to be the next great detective. He watched cartoons until he was out of high school and still prefers them over the horribly over-exaggerated programs that air these days.

His hands are trembling, not knowing what to do or where to seek help. He slides the car into the station and races inside to speak with Lucille. She is the only other person he trusts with the information and she has been working at the station since Stuart was a child. She would know what to do.

Lucille is sitting at her desk, sorting through files and forms as if today was a typical Saturday. Little does the elderly woman know that this Labor Day weekend has gotten off to an eerie start. "Lucille, when was the last time you heard from Sloane or Mitch? Have they called in at all today?"

Lucille Pennington looks up startled. She had been so engrossed in her work that she hadn't heard Stuart walk in. "Well hello there, young man. I haven't heard from either of them all day. What's the matter?"

"The last time I heard from Mitch was before he went to the mayor's business yesterday afternoon. I tried to reach him several times last night and this morning and was unable to get ahold of either of them." He pauses long enough to grab a bottle of water from the mini-fridge in the corner. "I went there this morning, to the mayor's place, and I saw some strange things." He continues to tell Lucille about the herd of poorly dressed and dirty foreigners he saw along the road, about the fallen trailer and the squad car that was left unattended. Lucille gasps for air when Stuart tells her he saw Sloane being pulled into the building by one of the Arroyo brothers.

"What are you going to do Deputy?" Even though Lucille is far older than he is, she still insists on calling all the officers by their title rather than their real name. "It seems to me like you are the only one that can help them. Did you call for help from the F.B.I. in Portland?"

Stuart tells her that they were already sending a team in to investigate what happened to the senior Mr. Billings, but that the team would only be evidence techs. He grabs a phone and places the call anyway, hoping that by some slim chance they may have sent a few field agents as well. He is informed rather quickly that most of the agents are tied up with some bomb threat made near the soccer stadium in Portland. Stuart hangs up and tells himself that is another reason why he hates soccer.

"No luck," he tells Lucille. "All their folks are tied up in something else."

She looks at him solemnly. "Looks like it's up to you. I know this isn't really in your ball park, but you are the only hope that Deputy Nichols and Sheriff Thompson have. They are counting on you."

He knows the older woman is right, even if he hates hearing it. He can't stop his hands from shaking. Going in alone against these three men would be suicide. Stuart knows that. He also knows there is only one person who is well trained enough to be successful against these killers. The trick will be getting the man to help. He is not a sworn officer and is a wanted man for what happened at Graham Park a few months back.

"Lucille, do we know where Ms. Reynolds is today? Is she still in town or did her party leave after the press conference? More importantly, do we know if any of her security detail is still in town?"

The questions confuse the older lady. "I'm not really sure. I don't see how that information would help with our situation."

"Let me worry about that. Can you make a few calls and see if you can find out anything? I know you are always current on the gossip in town." He leaves the lady to call whoever oversees the spreading of rumors around town, and heads to his desk to do a little online research on the man he needs.

The online resume of Jesse Meyers is readily available. After the incident in the amusement park, several websites popped up that were dedicated to the former Army Ranger. These sites are updated daily with fan sightings, most of them farfetched, and people claiming they saw him drive past them on the highway. Stuart scrolls past the numerous comments, looking for any indication that someone has seen him here in Twisted Timbers. He is not surprised that there is no mention of the town, or better yet, he is elated to see that no one has put the pieces together that Jesse Meyers is now Ethan Ward and is working for Ms. Reynolds, and that he was all over the television a few days ago. This means that the disguise and new name have done the trick and the former soldier may be more willing to help.

Stuart keeps one eye on his computer screen while constantly checking on Lucille. He is waiting for the older woman to motion to him that she has some information on where to find his man. He tried to get her to find the status of the security team for Ms. Reynolds without letting on the real identity of the one man he was seeking. Minutes go by, Lucille hanging up the phone and then dialing another number, Stuart still sitting at his desk waiting for the outcome.

After about an hour she motions him over. "It looks like the Reynolds family decided to stay in town for the weekend festivities. They were seen playing mini-golf just this afternoon and according to Blanche at the beauty salon, the mother had several scrumptious body guards with her."

"Does Blanche know where they might be now?" Stuart of course knows who Blanche is. He knows everybody in town. He also knows that Blanche spends more time staring out the window of her shop than she does working on hair. This trait makes her the most reliable source he can think of.

"She wouldn't swear to it, but her best guess is they stopped and had some ice cream before taking a hike on Eagle Ridge."

Stuart gets a big grin on his face. "Lucille, I could practically kiss you. Let Blanche know that she is now my favorite blue haired lady in all of town!" He says no more, just hurries through the big glass doors and gets into his squad car. His next mission is to figure out how to convince Jesse Meyers, or Ethan Ward, to help save Sloane and the Sheriff.

Chapter 32

All three of the Mexican men have retreated to the inner office. Sloane and Mitch sit in near silence for a few minutes, the only sound that can be heard is her soft whimpering. Mitch has no idea what to do. He knows he is supposed to comfort her, he loves this woman after all, but he has no answer. He has no idea how they are going to get out of here. He tries the simplest attempt to get her tears to stop, "I love you."

These words work, albeit briefly, and she replies. "I love you too. What are we going to do?"

It takes him far longer than it should to reply. He wants to be strong for her, but he is also a realist. Mitch knows that this woman is too smart and will see right through any bullshit answer he may try to make up on the fly. "I don't know." It's not the best answer, but it's the truth. "You know I thought you were dead." Now he is the one fighting back the urge to cry.

"I came very close," she proceeds to tell him all about the events of the previous afternoon. How she saw the flashing lights of the explosive device and decided saving the lives of the people in the trailer was more important than saving her own. How she screwed up and forgot to lower the legs on the trailer, causing it to tip forward, and how she lost focus and drove the large truck right off the side of the hill and had to jump from the moving vehicle. About waking up on the side of the hill, unaware of what had happened, lucky to still be alive.

"I've never been so happy to see someone walk through the door, even if you were being dragged. Trust me, I won't let anything happen to you." He tries to put up a strong façade, that he has everything under control. They both know he does not. "Were you able to reach out to Stuart for help? Does he know what's going on?"

"No. My phone busted when I went tumbling down the hill, and you left the squad car turned on and now it's dead. The radio was of no use." She neglects to tell him that she had the shotgun when she was caught and that she was disarmed rather easily, some things are just not worth mentioning to your superior officer, even if he is you lover.

"Stuart is a smart cop, he'll figure it out. What he lacks in bravery, he more than makes up for with brains." Mitch has known Deputy Johnson far longer than Sloane has, but it still sounds like he is trying to convince himself that Stuart will somehow get them out of here.

"What about you? Are you alright?"

"I'm fine. Just a few cuts and bruises. If we get out of this, I may need some stitches. The mayor, on the other hand, he may need a few days in the hospital before going to prison."

"Fill me in. Why is the mayor going to prison?" Once again Sloane shows the side of her that is always ready for action, no matter how dangerous things are or how bleak the current predicament. This is one of the things about her that Mitch finds the most appealing.

He begins to tell her about everything he has learned since being tied up. He tells her how the mayor made some sort of deal with The Butcher and then tried to steal from the Mexican. Part of what he is telling her is based on assumption, the rest he has been able to piece together. He also tells her how ruthlessly the Mexican has tortured Harry Billings and the intentions of the trio to blow up the entire town, probably at the parade tomorrow. He explains the large bomb that he saw on the desk in the office, to which Sloane replies that it sounded exactly like the explosive device that was in the truck she drove down the side of the cliff.

The two take a moment to catch their breath and grasp the enormity of the situation. Neither of them has any experience dealing with criminals of this magnitude or crimes as serious as drug smuggling or human trafficking. They are prisoners and have little hope of doing anything to stop the outcome. The only person that has a chance to save them is not exactly overflowing with bravery. The entire town could be in danger if these men follow through with their plan, and if their past behavior is any indication, they fully intend to follow through.

"Mitch." Her voice cuts through the silence. There is fear and panic, two things he has never heard from her before. "Do you think they will rape me?"

Once again, he is at a loss for words. This is a fear that only females have. Every female officer has probably thought about being captured and raped on at least one occasion. Mitch, much like every other male police officer, has never even pondered it happening to them. "I won't let that happen. They will have to kill me before they can do that."

"That's the problem. I don't think they would think twice about killing you." Again, her tears start up.

"That's not how this guy operates. You saw how he was when you first came in here. He wanted me to see him touching you. He wanted to see my reaction. He gets his thrills by the pain he causes to others, not the pain he causes to you. He is a true psycho. He wants to see your reaction as he terrorizes someone you love"

"I'm not sure that makes me feel any better. I don't want his hands on me and those other two guys are even more disgusting." Her tears have subsided, and her voice has more rage in it now, exactly how Mitch likes it. An angry and irritated Sloane will be more beneficial to their predicament than one who feels helpless and needy.

"Like I said, I won't let anything happen to you. Besides, I don't really think you are his type."

"What do you mean?"

He decides to break a little of the tension with his best defense, humor. "I think our Mexican friend prefers his lovers to be of the four-legged variety."

Chapter 33

The streets of town are full, much fuller than any Labor Day that Stuart Johnson can remember. Traffic is at a stand-still on Main Street, causing the deputy to use his flashing lights and siren to maneuver through the crowded streets. Most visitors are courteous and do their best to move out of the way, while others act like they have never seen a police car before. Several shop owners even come out of their businesses to see what the commotion is all about, the sirens being an odd sound in such a small, peaceful town, and Stuart still takes the time to wave to the ones he sees to reassure them that everything is alright.

It takes him nearly twice as long as it should to reach the start of the Eagle Ridge trail, even with the lights and siren. The normally mild-mannered Stuart has banged his hand on the steering wheel several times, honked his horn repeatedly and even called one oblivious driver a butt munch, which he instantly regrets. He knows that if his mother heard him say that, even if it is timid language to most humans, she would scold him relentlessly.

Like the rest of town, the parking lot to the hiking trail is packed. He circles the lot twice before deciding to leave the lights running and create his own parking spot in the grass near the road. This again is out of character for the deputy, but he doesn't have time to waste. He notices the dark SUV's parked side by side in the corner and heads straight for them. He knocks on the doors and windows of both cars, hoping that someone in the security detail for Ms. Reynolds would still be inside. Unfortunately, neither car is running, and no one answers his knocks. There's nothing left to do but start up the trail in search of Jesse Meyers.

The beginning of the trail is flat, with winding curves and a dense foliage canopy. The shade makes the temperature several degrees cooler than in the sunlight, something Stuart is thankful for. He hasn't visited any of the trails or stepped foot in the woods around town since he lost his partner, Jerome Carter, several weeks ago. He tries to put the events that happened back then out of his mind and focus on the task at hand, finding Jesse Meyers and convincing the man to help him save the sheriff and Deputy Nichols.

It doesn't take long for Stuart to run into the group of bodyguards that surround Ms. Reynolds. The men are so big that it's hard to get around them and keep your feet on the path. He steps aside enough for the first few to get by but when he spots Jesse Meyers near the back of the group, he motions to the former soldier that he wants to talk to him. Jesse Meyers keeps walking as if he hadn't seen Stuart.

The deputy races to keep pace, staying a few feet behind the group as they make their way back to the parking lot. He runs to his squad car while keeping one eye on his target and takes note of which SUV the man enters. Stuart starts the engine, puts the car into drive and accelerates quickly through the grass. He stops inches from the back bumper of the car that Jesse Meyers had gotten in and leaves his siren whaling.

The rear window comes down as the deputy approaches it, and Jesse looks out at him. "What can we do for you officer?"

"Can I speak to you in private?" Stuart is trying to get a look inside the vehicle. He had been so focused on which car that Jesse got in to he hadn't noticed if it was the same car Ms. Reynolds occupies as well.

"What is this about?" The man speaks out of the car in a neutral tone, but his eyes look at Stuart with spite.

"I'll explain, but let's go talk in private." Stuart knows that getting the man away from Ms. Reynolds, and more importantly, alone, will be the best chance he has to convince him to help. Jesse Meyers is the kind of person that would not let his primary objective fail in order to accomplish a secondary objective, even if the life of two officers were in jeopardy.

There was a bit of silence, Stuart just looking at the man and giving him his best pleading look. The silence is broken when Jesse speaks into the microphone that had been attached to his earpiece. Apparently, Ms. Reynolds had heard the conversation and urged her lead security officer to get out of the car and handle the business so that the family would not be held up any longer. Stuart steps away from the SUV and moves his vehicle enough to allow Jesse to get into the passenger seat and the security vehicle to safely exit the parking lot.

"I don't like being bothered when I'm working. Ms. Reynolds is very important to me and so is my job.

You better have a good reason for making a scene like that." The man speaks with a booming voice, one that makes Stuart think that convincing this man to do anything will be impossible.

"Sheriff Thompson is in trouble and I need help." Once again, using his most desperate voice.

"What does that have to do with me? I am not a cop. I am in no way affiliated with any law enforcement agency. You came out here and delayed my employer because you can't do your job?" The man is growing angrier by the minute and Stuart fears he will reach for the car door and be out of here if he doesn't do something.

"It's the Arroyo Brothers. For all I know, it could be El Carnicero too." He sees the former soldier perk up when he hears the names. "Mitch was last seen going out to the mayor's property yesterday afternoon with Deputy Nichols. Neither of them had reported in and I got worried this morning when I still couldn't contact them."

"I warned him about the Arroyo brothers on Thursday night. I told him there was something going on with the mayor." Jesse Meyers shakes his head at the stupidity of Sheriff Thompson for not having headed the warning. "I told him they were violent and crazy. I told him he needed to be careful."

"That's why I need your help." Maybe the soldier is starting to come around and see the urgency of the problem.

"I would love to help, but I have too much to lose. If the sheriff was stupid enough to get himself into a mess like this, then it's on him. I'm not sure why I should risk everything I have to help him."

The air turns silent. Stuart is lost. He is trying to figure out what, if anything he can say to change this man's mind. The two men look intently at each other. Stuart has to say something, but Jesse is so close to walking away, and if he does, it would seal the fate of both Mitch and Sloane.

"If there's nothing else deputy, I think I need to be going now." Jesse Meyers opens the passenger side of the patrol car and begins to exit. He is returning to the SUV that had obviously not been carrying Ms. Reynolds as it had stayed behind, waiting for the return of the head security officer.

Stuart tries to think of something quickly. He runs through everything he can remember about the man. He remembers seeing the description of him on the website that aired the game at Graham Park. The former soldier was the only one of the participants that had been given a nickname, and this name gives Stuart an idea. He presses the button and rolls down the passenger window.

His plan could go one of two ways. Either it works and persuades the man to help him rescue his colleagues, or it angers the man to the point where he kills Stuart with his bare hands. He decides he needs to try it, regardless of the outcome. "There are three Mexicans doing horrible things to two police officers, two American police officers, and you are walking away. Is this why they call you The Patriot?"

Jesse Meyers, or Ethan Ward, whatever you decide to call him, stops in his tracks. In online forums, people spoke of the former Ranger in high regard, like he was bigger than life. That he stood for everything good and holy. That he would never allow the persecution or harming of innocent Americans if he was in a position to stop it. Stuart had banked on these rumors being true. He counted on it.

Jesse walks back to the squad car slowly. Stuart stares at his face, hoping to get a gauge on how the man took his attempt at an insult. The soldier shows no sign, either way, but continues the slow methodical march toward the window. When he reaches the door, he bends in far enough to get his head in through the window. He looks at the older deputy for several minutes, his eyes piercing and sharp, before beginning to speak.

"Meet me on the road to the mayor's property at sunset. We would be sitting ducks if we tried anything in the daylight."

Stuart quickly replies, "meet you there? I'm not sure I would be much help."

Jesse Meyers laughs slightly, which makes Stuart uneasy. "What's the matter? Aren't you an American? Or are you just too chicken shit?"

Chapter 34

Sheriff Thompson had either fallen asleep or passed out, it's hard to tell which. The pain from the slash wounds on his chest is the first thing that causes him to awake. The second thing is the crying coming from the table where the mayor has been forced to endure his torture. Mayor Billings has taken a brutal beating at the hands of the three Mexicans, and for the last few hours he has been unconscious. He cries now, but even his tears lack much energy.

"Sloane?" He can't turn his head enough to see her, but he can still feel her hands pressed and tied against his own. She too has been silent for the last few hours. They talked sparingly in the last few moments before Mitch either fell asleep or passed out, mostly about the plans The Butcher shared for the town and the things the mayor was involved in that brought these men here.

Sloane tried to come up with ideas as to how they could get untied. Mitch can feel the rawness of the skin at his wrists from twisting his hands, trying to break through the ropes. They had no success. They both agreed to save what little energy they had in case of a rescue attempt from Stuart Johnson, even though they both knew that was unlikely.

He can see the dark shadows through the frosted glass that separates the warehouse from the office. He hasn't seen, or taken a beating from, any of the men since they left the warehouse shortly after tying them up. He wonders what they could be doing but is also thankful for the extra time, hoping it has bought them enough for the cavalry to arrive.

"I'm here. How are you feeling?" Her voice is soft and childlike, obviously the feeling of defeat has set in.

"I'm doing fine. I'm sorry, I must have passed out or something. Have they come out here lately?"

He feels her soft hand on his own and she squeezes it, not hard, but just enough to let him know she's there with him. "I haven't seen them. Can I tell you something?"

"Sure. You can tell me anything." Mitch braces for the worst.

"I've been thinking about it. I know you said you won't let them do anything to me, and that's sweet.

It just doesn't look like there is much we can do to stop them from doing," she pauses briefly, trying to find the right words. "I just don't think either one of us will be able to stop them if they want to do things to me. What I'm trying to say is, I will not let them lay a hand on me. I would rather die than to have them do that. If given the opportunity, I will take my own life to stop them from doing that to me." She sobs loudly now.

Mitch doesn't know what to say. He feels like an idiot. This woman, this strong, powerful woman who he loves, has just opened her soul to him. While he was passed out, she is tied right next to him weighing the pros and cons between suicide and being raped by these men. What kind of man doesn't know what to say in a time like this? He returns her squeeze with one of his own and searches for the right words. "It will never come to that. I promise you."

As if on cue, the three Mexicans come out from the confines of the office. Mitch turns his head quickly to see them and feels the movement of Sloane as she does the same. Juan and Humberto exit first, each holding a similar looking explosive device as the one that was on the desk earlier. They hold them far away from their bodies and walk extremely carefully across the concrete floor before exiting out the side door to the warehouse and into the parking lot. Mitch is relieved to have the bombs far away from where they are sitting.

The Butcher ignores the two officers and makes his way over to the still sobbing Mayor Billings. Mitch watches as he uses his full body weight to pull on the lever for the vice that is still holding the right hand of the mayor. More bones cracking and breaking, more screams of agony and a slight chuckle from The Butcher. The crime boss walks slowly around the work bench eyeing the mostly naked body of the mayor. He stops at his over-sized midsection and pats his belly a few times, like he would pat the head of an obedient puppy.

Satisfied, El Carnicero turns his attention to Mitch and Sloane. His long strides cover the twenty or so feet to them in only a few steps. He stands between them, looking down on the lovers in disdain. The man disappears from Mitch's view, but he is still close enough that the sheriff can smell him, the cheap cologne, the cigar smoke and the arrogance all blend together in a putrid odor.

"What is a fine-looking thing like you doing in this shit town?"

No reply from Sloane.

"Aw. You don't want to talk to me? I like a girl that plays hard to get. It makes me have to work harder to get what I want, but I always get it eventually."

Mitch can hear the man talking to Sloane. His Sloane. It infuriates him. He tries again to tug at his bindings. It seems that every time he pulls against them, they get tighter on his wrists.

"Get away from her!" He tries to sound tough and imposing but his voice cracks mid-sentence and it comes out more like a little boy who is being held down by his older sibling.

"Ah. The brave boyfriend speaks again. I am an evil man, some even call me psychotic. But there is one thing I have never done. Do you know what that is Sheriff?"

Mitch can sense the man beginning to walk closer to him. While drawing the man's attention will probably cause more pain to himself, at least he has gotten him to stop focusing on Sloane. "Take a bath?"

This draws a hard slap from The Butcher, followed by a closed fist punch to his midsection. It knocks the air from the sheriff.

"Man. I can't decide if you are brave or just one stupid gringo. I have never taken advantage of a woman. Women in my country know who I am. That is all that is usually needed. I don't like the women in this country. They are all pigs if you ask me."

"That's because they have better taste in this country." This too draws a punch to the stomach from The Butcher. Mitch has always used his sense of humor as a way of diffusing a tense situation, but his wisecracks never caused as much pain as they do now.

"Let me ask you another question Sheriff Thompson. Do you know what they say is the most painful way to die?"

The topic of death is not what Mitch wants to be thinking about right now. He shakes his head as his only reply to the question.

"They say that burning to death is by far the most painful way to die. I had intended on killing your beloved mayor this way, but then you two decided to stick your noses in my business."

Mitch looks up at the man. "I thought you were going to use the bomb you showed me in the office."

El Carnicero laughs out loud. "Oh no. You were mistaken. The bombs you saw my men carrying are for the rest of the town. It should make the Labor Day festivities, how do you say, a year to remember. We have packed enough explosives onto the trucks they will use tomorrow to set this entire town on fire."

Mitch had heard him mention the parade earlier but hadn't tied the pieces together like The Butcher just had. He hears the door to the outside open again from behind him, but he keeps his gaze on the crazed Mexican.

"Like I was saying, I was going to kill your mayor by setting him on fire, but then you two butted in. Now I think I will let all three of you see what it's like to be burned to death. They say it is even more painful than giving birth."

Sloane gasps at this, followed closely by loud crying. Earlier she had just been sobbing, but now Mitch can hear her bellow in child-like cries. Humberto comes from around the other side, it must have been him who came in through the door earlier. He sets down two large gas cans in the area of concrete between the mayor's table and the two chairs.

Mitch watches the large man as he starts carrying large wooden pallets, three at a time, and begins stacking them around the two chairs and in piles between Mitch and the mayor. Humberto easily rips the wood slats apart like they are twigs, tossing pieces of sharp wood at the feet of the sheriff, tossing more on top of the lifeless body of the mayor. The man moves quickly, far faster than a man of his size should. He adds stacks of cardboard boxes to the pile, not wasting time removing any of the packing materials that may still be inside. In a matter of minutes, Humberto Arroyo has successfully turned the concrete floor of the warehouse into a garbage heap.

Mitch can see what Humberto is attempting to do. When you grow up surrounded by forests, you learn at a young age how to make a bonfire. At the rate he is going, Humberto Arroyo would qualify for his fire-making badge in a matter of seconds. What had been an open concrete floor just a few moments ago, now looks like the aftermath of a tornado.

The Butcher says something in Spanish and nods his approval at the big man's work. Humberto scurries passed the two deputies and Mitch can once again hear the door close behind him. He watches the older man struggle to raise one of the gas cans, presumably filled with diesel fuel since they are at a trucking complex, and begin pouring the liquid all over the wood and cardboard that now covers the floor. He circles the table where the mayor is lying and pours more fuel up and down his body. He circles back, giving a second coat of fuel to the heap of kindling in the middle of the floor before tossing away the empty plastic jug.

Mitch can smell the fumes of the diesel, he can almost taste it. The Butcher picks up the second can and pours a circle around the two chairs the officers are tied in. He makes two complete loops around them, getting closer with every step. "You know, when we first came to this town, I hated it. Then you two showed up and made it a little more fun." He finishes the sentence by dumping some of the fuel onto the head of Mitch and Sloane.

Mitch can feel it run down his back, drenching every inch of his clothing. He can hear Sloane trying to spit out the bits of the flammable liquid that must have gotten into her mouth. He can feel the vibrations as she tries to reach the man, her will to fight still active. He can hear the liquid hitting the concrete floor again, but the footsteps are also getting further away. Sloane has stopped the panicked attempts to get free.

"Where is he? Sloane, what's going on?"

"I don't know Mitch, but it's not good. He made a line to the door with the diesel fuel. Then he just walked out."

Mitch has watched enough movies to know this won't end up well. "He'll be back. They always come back."

Chapter 35

Stuart felt flustered as he made the short drive back the police station. He had wanted the former soldier to help, and Jesse agreed to help, but he also said Stuart would be coming along as well. He had hoped Jesse Meyers would take it upon himself to handle the situation. Surely, he knows the kind of reputation Deputy Johnson has. Anyone who has been in town for more than a day knows what kind of officer Stuart Johnson is, or rather, what kind of officer he is not.

The ride through town is even more congested with traffic than it was earlier in the afternoon. The hikers have all left the trails and have converged on the downtown area. It won't be long until the sun begins to set, and Stuart still feels the need to cover his entire body in Kevlar. He is racing through the streets, changing lanes as often as needed and even driving the wrong way down Main Street to avoid further delays.

He finally makes it to the station, parks the car and runs through the giant glass doors. He doesn't stop to greet Lucille Pennington who is still seated at her desk. He makes a straight line for the locker room and begins undressing. The Kevlar vest is heavy and cumbersome, that much Stuart remembers. What he doesn't remember was how little of the body the vest actually protected. Now knowing that he is going to have a confrontation with the three Mexicans, Stuart feels the vest is highly inadequate.

He puts the shirt over the vest, struggles with getting his arms through the sleeves and tucking the shirt back in, and heads to the ammo locker. The locker is where the department keeps the extra ammunition and the weapons that carry higher fire power, like rifles and shotguns. He doesn't know what he should bring and picks up one of the shotguns. He feels the weight in his hands and puts the large gun back on the shelf. Next, he holds one of the long hunting rifles. He's fired rifles several times while hunting for deer, but again decides the gun would be too large to allow him to remain hidden if needed. Extra firepower would be the right choice if he were an officer who was willing to use the weapon, but Stuart is not that kind of officer. He settles on two extra magazines for his police issued handgun and slams the door to the locker closed.

Before leaving the locker room, Deputy Johnson looks at himself in the full-length mirror on the back side of the door. His white uniform top is not going to make it easy to hide in the shadows, so he grabs a pullover hoodie from his locker. The sweatshirt is black and clashes with his dark blue uniform slacks, but he is not worried about how he looks and is more focused on his ability to remain hidden throughout the course of the night. He looks at himself in the mirror once more and is happy to see that the only thing he will need to worry about keeping hidden is his face. He contemplates using a black marker to darken his skin but decides that would be going too far.

He sprints from the locker room and right past Lucille again. He doesn't want to fill her in on the situation. The lady worries too much about the officers and their safety. If she were to find out that Mitch and Sloane were captured by three Mexican men who have a long history of murder and violence, she wouldn't stop trying to find a way to save them, even calling on the Army for help, if she could. As he exits the building, Stuart looks up at the sky. The sun is nearly beyond the horizon, turning what had been a magnificently blue sky into one filled with oranges and pinks that look like paint strokes as they bleed through the clouds.

Travelling south out of town is far less chaotic. It takes just a few minutes to reach the stretch of road that follows the river through all its winds and turns and past where the foreigners were spotted walking earlier in the afternoon. He turns off the lights of his patrol car before he reaches the opening to the trucking company lot and slides his car behind the deserted car that Sheriff Thompson left parked on the side of the road. Branches from the low-hanging trees screech against the window and roof of the car as he slides the transmission into neutral.

As he gets out of the car, the silence of the night makes his surroundings creepier than he would have liked. He has been to the trucking company lot a few times, but never with the cloud of danger lingering in the air like it is tonight. He begins to raise his flashlight from his belt, more out of habit, before he remembers the threat that could be only a few feet away. The Mexicans are here, or at least they were earlier, this much he is certain of. The thought of the three men makes him return the flashlight without shining the light and simply lean against his car.

Jesse Meyers had agreed to help him, and the man told him to meet him here at sunset. He was here a few minutes after the sun went down and there is no sign of the former soldier. Stuart leans against the trunk of his car, trying to see as much of the parking lot as he can while looking through the windows of both police cars. It's hard to make out anything, but Stuart is happy to just stay where he is. If he can't see The Butcher or the Arroyo brothers, then they can't see him. If they can't see him, then he is safe.

It's natural in a wooded setting like this to hear sounds coming from areas which are too dark to see. Stuart would usually not be so jumpy, but with the combination of the events earlier in the year and the fact that he knows there are violent criminals nearby, has him a little more skittish than normal. He is continuously trying to shield his body with the frame of the car or massaging his chest where the straps of the Kevlar vest dig repeatedly into his slight body.

It's now been ten minutes since he arrived and there is still no sign of Jesse Meyers. Stuart is left weighing his options. On one hand, Mitch and Sloane are in trouble. They need him. On the other hand, the people holding his fellow officers are world renowned for being violent and good at what they do. If he were to walk in there alone, he would be no match for the trio of Mexicans. He knows this. He knows all of this. His heart is torn. His mind is torn. His body is the only part of him that is decisive and it will not allow the man to move from his hiding spot.

Chapter 36

For the most part, the warehouse is silent. The Butcher left a few minutes ago and since then neither of the officers have said a word. There are no sounds coming from the mayor either. Mitch thinks the mayor may have decided to take the easy way out and quit fighting when he heard the intentions of the Mexican. There has also been very little coming from behind Mitch, where Sloane is also tied to a chair. They both went through spouts of coughing and gagging from the nauseous fumes from the diesel fuel, but she has not said a word.

"Sloane, we have to try to get out of these ropes. Can you move your hands at all?"

The female deputy spits a few times, an action they have both done to avoid the putrid taste of the diesel from reaching their taste buds. "I've been trying. My hands are practically numb. What do you think the man is going to do?"

"I think he's a madman. I know he has two bombs that he is planning on using to blow up large portions of town during the parade, when the streets are full of tourists."

She cuts him off, "I know all of that. I mean, what do you think he is going to do with us?"

Mitch knows what the man intends to do, and he knows that Sloane knows as well. "I think we both know what he plans on doing. He covered us in diesel for a reason, and that path he poured that leads to the door is his way of assuring he doesn't get caught up in the blaze. He can light the fuel from over there and watch as it makes its way to us before escaping."

"Well that's just freaking great!"

"I'm not sure what you want me to do about it. As you can see, I'm tied up just as much as you are."

"I'm sorry Mitch. I didn't mean to raise my voice. I'm scared Honey."

Mitch doesn't know how to respond to this. Sloane is the last person who would ever be willing to admit that she is scared. On top of that, she never ever calls him by a pet name. The fact that she did tells him that her normally rock-solid façade is starting to crack. He takes another look at the mayor, but the man has not moved in the last few minutes. He tries again to wiggle his hands free but has no luck.

"Let's see if we can move together. Push your back against mine and I'll do the same. Maybe we can get far enough from this pile of wood that we won't ignite." He had no idea where this idea came from, but as he says it, Mitch begins to like the plan more.

"That's not going to work, you're bigger and stronger than I am."

"That doesn't matter. We don't have to get all the way to our feet, we just have to lift ourselves enough to get the legs of the chairs off the ground. Besides, it's not like you to walk away from a physical challenge."

Mitch knows the last line is all the extra encouragement Sloane will need. As if on cue, he can feel her using her legs to press her body as far backwards as she can. The sudden force against his body happens without warning, forcing his chair onto its front legs, almost causing the pair to tumble over. Mitch begins to use his legs to apply an equal amount of pressure against her back. The two bodies lift slightly off the seats of the wooden chairs.

"That's it. Keep pushing. Once we get the chairs up, we'll take small steps to the right." Mitch encourages her to give more, even as he hears her grunts of exertion.

"Wait. My right or your right?" Sloane says through gritted teeth.

Mitch almost bursts out laughing, "my right. Towards the office. Just a bit higher now."

The more they push their bodies against the back of the chairs and each other, the higher they begin to rise. Eventually the chairs leave the floor as well. Moving in synchronized motions that only a couple who is intimate could, they begin to move toward the office. Mitch is the first to kick a large chunk of wood, trying to clear his path. Sloane notices what he is doing and begins to kick pieces of cardboard as hard as she can.

From a distance, the two would look like an older couple, who are both suffering from severe back pain, trying to do some sort of ancient tribal dance ritual. Every time one of them kicks a piece of debris from their path, both chairs and the people in them sway from side to side. It takes every inch of energy Mitch has left in his body to stop them from falling.

When they clear the pile of kindling that Humberto Arroyo piled around them, they sit the chairs down gently. Both officers are sweating profusely and breathing heavily through their noses. Sheriff Thompson uses this time of relief to look around the open expanses of the warehouse. Now that they have mastered the ability to move about, he hunts for something that could cut through the ropes. He has no idea how much time they have before The Butcher comes back, so he searches the room frantically, at least as much of it as he can see.

He knows that every time one of the Mexicans got a tool, they got it from the far side of the room, the side opposite of where the mayor currently lays on the work table. The distance to get to that side of the room is far longer than what they just covered. If they had unlimited time, there is no doubt in his mind that they could make it. But they don't have unlimited time. They could have only a few seconds before The Butcher comes back and starts the barbecue.

"Sloane, how much energy do you have left? I have an idea but it's going to be tough."

Her hard-breathing stops, "I can do it." She doesn't ask what the plan is or complain about her situation. She simply says she's ready.

"I think if we make our way to the other side of the room, on the other side of Mayor Billings, we might be able to find a saw or something to cut the ropes."

Again, the pressure from Sloane rising out of her chair is almost enough to push him forward and pull them both down in a heap. It seems almost easier for them to get the chair legs off the floor this time. They begin the small steps toward the far side of the room as if they practice the maneuver on their nights at home alone. Mitch begins turning the pair slightly, so they can both see where they are headed. He gives loud, one-word commands to help the pair work in unison.

Mitch has made the decision to take the shortest path to where they are going, which is also the most difficult. He hopes that the shorter distance will give them enough time to find a tool to cut the ropes before the Mexican returns. The problem with the shorter route is that it requires them to cross through the same pile of debris that they fought hard to get out of in the first place.

They avoid the clearing where they were originally seated, and Mitch opts to usher them toward a spot in the debris that is less thick than most of the area around it. Only a few pieces of wooden skid and a couple of flattened cardboard boxes block them from getting to the needed tools. He lets Sloane know the area they are aiming for and again begins barking out the easy directional commands.

Mitch can feel his thighs burning. He knows that Sloane is in far better shape than he is and all her mornings of getting up early to go running are serving her well. It's also harder for Mitch because he is much larger than she is. He is slouched much lower, putting even more pressure on his thighs and calves to support the weight of the pair. Despite the pain, they have managed to negotiate their way back to the debris and trash that was thrown in the middle of the floor.

Mitch must raise his left leg higher than normal to step over a large piece of overturned wooden skid. This puts his body in a precarious position as the large step to his side means he must hold all his weight on a single leg while he waits for Sloane to take the two steps needed to catch up. Once both of his legs are over the wooden obstacle, he begins to relax. He takes his focus off the steps he needs to take and begins trying to check for useful tools that might be close by.

His steps are so small that he thinks it's almost impossible for him to trip. He continues to walk slowly, without looking at what's under his feet. He fails to see the last piece of cardboard box, covered in the diesel fuel, which is more slippery than Mitch had expected. His already weakened legs are unable to keep him upright and the pair tumble to the ground. They are now staring up at the ceiling, still tied together with their backs touching. Mitch can feel the wetness against his cheek from the small puddle of diesel that remains on the concrete where their bodies ended up.

"Are you alright?"

There was a brief pause before Sloane responded, "yeah I'm fine. We might be worse off now than we were before though."

She had barely gotten the words out when they both heard the door to the warehouse open. They banged heads together as each of them reacted to the sound, straining their heads to see the front door at the same time. The Butcher stands in the doorway, perplexed at the sight of the two officers laying on the ground ten feet from where he left them. His laughter echoes through the large open room, bouncing from one wall to the next before piercing the ears of the fallen Sheriff Thompson.

Mitch watches as El Carnicero shakes the thick cigar that he pulls from his pants pocket. The man raises the cigar to his mouth and bites the end before lighting it with a silver lighter he pulls from the same pocket. Mitch wants to look away, not wanting to see the moment the crazed man puts flame to the fuel, but he is also holding out hope that someone will come to their rescue. He is holding out hope that Stuart will somehow come racing in and save them. His hopes are dashed when The Butcher flicks the lighter and the flame sprouts from the top, turning the end of the cigar into a bright orange ember. A bright orange ember that could easily set this entire room ablaze, and there's nothing Mitch can do to stop it.

Chapter 37

The night is completely dark, and the peacefulness and serenity has made Stuart more tired than he should be. He is still leaning against his squad car awaiting the arrival of Jesse Meyers, the former soldier. He has been standing here for nearly an hour and has not heard a single sound that he would consider out of place. The night air is beginning to cool down and even though he wore it for different reasons, he is glad to have the hooded sweatshirt on. To pass time while he has been waiting, Stuart has tried to use his binoculars to search the parking lot of the trucking company for the Mexican men. He hasn't seen them or caught a sign of either of the missing officers.

It's not out of character for Stuart to stand around and do nothing. Much of his time on the clock is spent standing at one corner or another directing traffic. Rarely though, is he ever left to stand around in the dark, without seeing another vehicle for this long. He decides he will get on the car radio and see if Lucille has heard from either of the missing deputies. As he approaches the driver side door, he hears a soft sound in the distance.

It's hard for him to make out the sound and he was probably too far away from it when he was at the rear of his vehicle. He inches closer, keeping his eyes fixed on the opening to the parking lot. The sound is coming from the direction of the second police car. Mitch's police car. He still has no idea what the sound could be but as he gets nearer, he can begin to make out words. He had parked as close to the other car as he could, so the distance to the back bumper is less than a few feet. When he gets to the rear of Mitch's car, he sees a tiny headset placed neatly on the shiny metal trunk.

He had not seen it when he pulled in, mainly because he turned off his headlights long before reaching this part of the roadway. He picks up the small earpiece and places it his ear. Right away he can hear the unmistakable voice of Jesse. "Stuart, if you can hear me, please respond." Stuart attaches the clip to his belt and presses the small button before responding.

"I'm here. I've been here for an hour."

"Ok. Listen carefully. I need you to proceed into the parking lot."

"Wait!" Stuart was scared enough thinking he would be with the Army soldier when they made their way into the parking lot, now he is being asked to walk in alone. "I thought you were going to help me. Where are you?"

"Don't worry about that. If you follow my instructions, you'll be fine. I am nearby." The former Ranger speaks in soft but firm words. "I need you to make your way toward the blue box trailer. Do you see it?"

Stuart remembers seeing the blue trailer when he first pulled to the shoulder of the road. It's the trailer that is furthest away from the building and closest to where he is now standing. "I saw it earlier. I know where it's at."

"Good. Stay low and make your way there. When you get there, I'm going to need you to crab walk under it and lie down on your stomach."

"You do realize I'm not a soldier. That I've never been a soldier. I can get under the trailer and lie down, but I have no idea what a crab walk is." He waits for a long period, but no reply comes over the ear piece.

Stuart begins inching along the side of Mitch's car, trying to make his tall and gangly body as small as possible. His feet pick up speed when he gets to the area past the car, where he is completely exposed. There is fifteen feet or so where he will be unprotected, and he forces himself to refrain from sprinting, knowing it will make too much noise as his feet hit the gravel. His heart is in his throat for the entirety of the trip.

Once he reaches the blue trailer, he quickly falls to his stomach and slides his body under the frame. The Kevlar vest acts as protection from the gravel as he forces his body between the trailer tires. Once he believes he is in the center of the trailer he uses the button on the radio and lets Jesse knows he is in position. He rolls over on his back, looking up at the underside of the trailer and the rusted metal. He waits several minutes but no response comes. He tries again.

Before he can finish his sentence into the microphone, he feels the body of another man slide under the trailer next to him. Jesse is dressed in full dark camouflage and his face is painted black. Stuart has an odd sense of realization that the soldier looks far better in his face makeup than he would have if he had used a marker. Neither man says a word for a long time. The silence is broken when Jesse turns and looks at Stuart, the soldier's eyes covered by the bulky lenses of night optics.

"I know you can't see them, but the Arroyo boys are in the lot, one at three and the other at nine."

Jesse Meyers is on his stomach and looking toward the building where Stuart last saw Deputy Nichols. Trying to see what the soldier is looking at, Stuart rolls onto his stomach, less smoothly than he would have liked. He pulls his binoculars to his eyes, but the night is too dark, and the area is not very well lit. No matter how many times he adjusts the lenses, he can't see anything other than dark shadows. He drops the binoculars and looks at the former soldier. The man yanks the cheap binoculars from the deputy and shoves a much heavier pair into his hands. Stuart raises them to his eyes and is mesmerized by the sharp contrast of the objects in the parking lot.

"Juan is at the truck at three, he's throwing stuff out of the cab."

"Three?" Stuart is left dumbfounded by the use of military jargon. He notices Jesse nodding his head to the left and looks in that direction. "Why do you have to make it so difficult. Couldn't you just say left?"

Jesse doesn't respond so Stuart decides to focus his attention on the truck to his left, nearest the rear of the building. The clarity of the lenses he is looking through make it easy for him to see there is a figure inside the truck. He can't make out facial details, but he can see the top of the person's head pop up from time to time over the dashboard. He scans the area around the truck, and he can see the items that were discarded, just like the soldier said.

"You stay here and keep an eye out for the other subject interfering. I'm going to go take of Juan, when I give you the signal, I need you to come to where I am. Got it?"

Stuart is more than happy to stay hidden under the truck while the soldier does the dirty work. "I got it. I stay here and you take out the Arroyo boys."

"No Stuart. I will take care of Juan, but when I do, I need you to come and keep him down while I handle Humberto. He's likely to be a problem."

Stuart shakes his head adamantly, trying to convince the shoulder to reconsider the plan. "I can't do that! What if something goes wrong and I'm out in the open?"

"Nothing is going to go wrong. I've done these things before. Just stay low when you make your way across the parking lot. If we're lucky, Humberto will never know we are there, and I will still be able to sneak up on him."

He knows that Jesse Meyers was a professional soldier at one time in his life, but this doesn't make Stuart feel at ease. He takes a moment to look down at the gravel and try to gather the inner strength from places of his body he has never searched for it. When he raises his head back up, and looks to his side, Jesse Meyers is no longer lying next to him. Deputy Johnson fumbles for the binoculars the soldier had given him and presses them against his face.

He can make out the former soldier as he walks delicately toward the truck with the open door, on the left side of the building. Stuart can feel his anxiety build as Jesse inches closer. He has no idea how the man is going to be able to subdue Juan Arroyo without causing enough commotion that Humberto comes to his brothers' rescue. Jesse hadn't really divulged that information.

Stuart watches as the former Army Ranger moves like a scared cat, letting his boots contact the gravel softly before allowing his body weight to come down fully. Jesse works his way along the side of the trailer, his steps becoming more methodical the closer he gets to the cab of the truck. Stuart looks on, thankful to still be hidden and feeling like he has the best seat in the house for the upcoming action.

Jesse's slow steps become even slower, inching nearer to the cab, before he leaps onto the bottom step. He throws his hands inside the truck and shakes his arms violently from side to side. Stuart is at first surprised by the quickness of the soldier, he hadn't been prepared for the attack. From his position under the trailer, all that he can see is the backside of Jesse, but the action taking place inside looks violent.

After a few seconds, Jesse Meyers backs himself out of the cab of the truck, dragging the near lifeless body of Juan Arroyo behind him. He waves his hands toward Stuart, who takes a deep breath before crawling through the gravel. When he clears the edge of the trailer, Stuart gets to his feet. He suddenly becomes aware that he is out in the open and hurries his strides. The weight of the Kevlar vest and the unsure footing on the gravel lot causes him to be even more clumsy than he usually is.

His increased momentum has taken his body forward, quicker than he had expected. He urges his feet to move faster and catch up to his upper body, hoping to get his balance back. Unfortunately, gravity has grabbed ahold of his upper body, forcing him to lean forward at the waist. Stuart knows what is coming and manages to steal a glance at the former Ranger, who looks at the deputy with disappointment. Stuart crashes to the ground in a large racket, the weight of his vest displacing gravel as the soles of his boots spit more rocks flying about. What was intended to be a stealth attack has now turned into a full-volume assault.

"Well that's one way to make an entrance. Put this guy in cuffs." Jesse releases the hands of Juan Arroyo and allows the deputy to take over.

"I'm sorry. I warned you that I wasn't much of a soldier." Stuart is embarrassed and doesn't want to look Jesse in the eyes. "Let's just hope that the other one didn't hear me."

"I doubt there's any chance of that, although there may be some folks down in San Francisco who didn't hear you."

The two men finally look at each other. Stuart has climbed down and placed a knee into the back of the smaller Mexican brother. He looks up at Jesse, apologetic at first, but when he sees the small grin on the face of the man, he relents and smiles back. Once the handcuffs are secure, Stuart climbs to his feet and stands beside the soldier. "That was pretty impressive. I've never seen someone move like that."

"The Army trained me pretty well." Jesse turns and looks in the direction of the second brother. The truck he was in is barely visible from the side of the lot they are in. Neither of them needed to have a visual on the truck or Humberto Arroyo to know that the bigger man knew that his brother was in trouble or had been captured.

The rumbling comes low and deep. Stuart at first thinks he is hearing a storm roll in from the ocean. It isn't until Jesse Meyers takes off in a dead sprint that he realizes the sound he hears is that of the truck starting up. Stuart takes a few steps to follow Jesse, looks back at Juan on the ground and decides that he would be best served to stay here and secure the prisoner. He places his knee on the fallen man's back and brings the night-vision binoculars back to his eyes. The truck has circled the lot and moves slowly through the gravel. Jesse is chasing after it, arms pumping like cylinders. Stuart has no idea what the man intends to do, but he can't take his eyes off him. As he closes the distance, it's obvious that the driver of the truck, Humberto Arroyo, is attempting to drive the thing away.

There is more than likely a bomb in the truck and Jesse Meyers is the only chance they have of keeping the bomb away from town. If the maniac got away, and somehow managed to get the truck into town, the damage could be catastrophic. A few days ago, Stuart was wondering if he should walk up to the soldier while he was on stage at the press conference and arrest the man. Now he watches the man and is silently cheering for him to succeed. He hears small grumblings coming from the prisoner below his body, but the view from the binoculars is the only thing Stuart is focused on.

Jesse is moving like a natural athlete. He is able to get closer to the truck every time the driver tries to change gears. Humberto doesn't grind the gears like Sloane did when she drove the other truck, but he is not as fluid as a person who drives a truck for a living. The slow shifting allows the pursuer to close the distance. As the driver finally points the nose of the truck toward the exit to the lot, Jesse Meyers makes a lung for the gap between the truck and trailer.

Jesse is only out of sight for a few seconds, Deputy Johnson watches as the trailer begins to shake violently, followed by smoke coming from the tires. Jesse Meyers flies through the air and tumbles to the ground, completing a full somersault before landing on his feet. When the truck comes to a complete stop, Stuart can see the red and blue air lines dangling from the truck. Stuart grins. In a moment as tense as this one, Jesse Meyers was able to think clearly enough to know that the inexperienced driver would not know how to handle it if the airlines were suddenly disconnected. Without proper airflow, the trailer brakes would engage and lock up the rear wheels. The deputy concedes that if it were him chasing the truck, he wouldn't have thought to disconnect the airlines.

There is more mumbling from Juan Arroyo but it only forces Deputy Johnson put more weight onto the small man's back. His eyes are glued to Jesse Meyers, who stands near the truck waiting on Humberto Arroyo. It isn't long before the massive Mexican obliges and exits the truck. The two men look at each other, each judging the strength of their opponent. They circle each other, each man moving to his left. From where he sits, Stuart thinks the matchup resembles a school bully picking on a much smaller kid. As if a mythical bell rung, the two men charge at each other at the same time.

Chapter 38

Humberto Arroyo may be much bigger than Jesse Meyers, but the former soldier has the speed advantage. As they charge toward each other at full speed, Jesse takes a small step to his left, using his right leg to trip the big man. There was no force in the trip, but the size and momentum of Humberto were both working against him. He fell to his knees on the gravel and looked over his shoulder at Jesse, who had circled like a prize fighter and placed a perfectly timed right hand to the chin of the downed man.

Jesse looks possessed, landing punches and kicks to the big man in rapid succession. Stuart thought he would kill the man, who was still on his knees on the gravel. After an especially strong kick to the abdomen, Jesse sets up to deliver another heavy boot to the face of the Mexican. Humberto anticipates the kick and grabs Jesse by the leg and flips him on his back. The larger man moves quick and climbs on top of the soldier.

Humberto Arroyo doesn't deliver as many blows as Jesse had, but his strikes carry more force. He drops heavy blows to the head of Jesse Meyers and smiles while he does it. Humberto pauses briefly, only long enough to spit out a stream of blood, a result of the damage he took earlier. When he returns to throwing haymakers at the smaller Jesse, Humberto lacks urgency. He is surprised when the soldier begins to fight back once again.

It's obvious in the look in the Mexican's face that he is not used to his victims surviving his powerful assaults. The two men are now rolling through the gravel, taking turns being on top of the other with each of them throwing random punches and kicks. Stuart once again feels like he should do something to help the soldier, but every time he relaxes and removes his weight from Juan, the man attempts to escape. Jesse made it very clear that Stuart was tasked with keeping Juan under control while he handled the larger of the brothers. He vows to not leave the man and allow him to get away.

The two men continue to wrestle. At one point, Stuart was convinced that Humberto was choking the life out of Jesse. They were frozen in the same position for a few seconds, Jesse on his back and Humberto perched above him. In the darkness, Stuart was unable to see that Jesse had his thick legs wrapped around the man's neck, cutting off the air flow. Jesse increased the pressure on the man's neck, causing him to pass out from lack of oxygen.

The limp body of the once imposing Humberto Arroyo falls to the ground. Seconds later, Jesse Meyers stands and shakes out his arms and legs, dusting off his clothing in the process. He reaches down and grabs the legs of the passed-out Humberto. He struggles to drag the massive body across the gravel, stopping several times to catch his breath and get a better grip. Once he drags the body close to the truck, Jesse pulls out handcuffs of his own and secures the big man to the front axle of the truck.

Jesse Meyers practically collapses on the step of the truck once Humberto is secure. This the first time that Stuart has seen the man breath heavily. Stuart decides to take a cue from the man and uncuffs the right hand of Juan. If he can cuff him to the truck like Jesse did with Humberto, then he can feel more comfortable about his situation. As soon as the cuff is taken off his hand, Juan spins around quickly and gives Stuart a knee to the stomach.

The man is quick, getting to his feet almost before Stuart felt the knee hit his midsection. He grasps for the Mexican, but the man is out of his reach. The vest he's been wearing eats much of the blow, but the force of the strike has taken his wind away. He hurries to his feet and begins to chase the man. Juan Arroyo turns his head to look behind him, but his eyes go past Stuart to something behind. Stuart has no idea what the man is looking at, but he stops in his tracks when Juan begins to scream.

"Enciende el fuego! Enciende el fuego!"

Stuart turns and follows the path of Juan's eyes, and catches sight of El Carnicero standing in the doorway of the warehouse. The crime boss has no idea what is going on in the parking lot and is apparently talking to whomever is still in the building, Mitch and Sloane, Stuart assumes. Stuart understands the foreign words that Juan has shouted, but it isn't until he sees the cigar in the mouth of The Butcher, and he catches the slight odor of diesel fumes that he can put the pieces together.

Jesse Meyers has noticed the commotion and has gotten up from where he was seated. The soldier does not move in a panic like Stuart had. He simply walks methodically through the gravel, slowly pulling his pistol from his hip holster. He raises it and takes aim, firing one shot that Stuart can practically feel buzz past his ear. The deputy turns and watches the body of Juan Arroyo crumble to the ground.

For the first time since he got here tonight, Stuart finally knows what he must do next. He knows what's going on. Jesse looks at him with puzzled eyes, but Stuart has no time to explain, he just barges past the Ranger, stopping only to grab one thing. One very important thing.

Chapter 39

El Carnicero, The Butcher, stands in the doorway and just looks down at the two fallen officers. He says nothing. Instead, he simply puffs on his cigar multiple times, allowing the smoke to escape his mouth in a slow steady stream. Mitch has his eyes glued to the man and watches as the cloud of smoke dances through the air before escaping to the rafters of the cavernous warehouse. The man has looked down on Mitch and Sloane for several seconds without saying a word. His look tells Mitch that he is searching for what he wants to do next.

After allowing the door to close softly behind him, The Butcher slowly walks through the room toward them. He is careful to not allow his feet to touch the parts of the floor that have been soiled from the diesel fuel. He kicks a few of the boards and pieces of wood back in to the larger pile near the pair of officers. He doesn't say anything to them, but he also doesn't take his eyes away from Mitch's. The man has a presence about him that oozes nastiness, the sight of him causing Mitch to wince in disgust.

He stops near them briefly, taking enough time to give a prolonged sniff near Sloane's body. Again, he doesn't say anything, but this time he gives out a grunt of approval. The old man rises back to his feet and makes his way to the body of Mayor Billings. Harry Billings hasn't moved in the last few minutes and Mitch has no idea if the man is still alive. He has been beaten repeatedly throughout the night and both his hand and knee has been crushed in the metal vice that is affixed to the corner of the table.

It's takes all the effort he can muster for Mitch to rotate their bodies in a manner so that he can keep his eyes on The Butcher. He was only able to adjust them properly once Sloane realized what he was trying to do and helped by rotating her hips. By looking over their heads, they can see The Butcher as he walks around the mayor's body. He makes several rotations around the work bench, stopping a few times to slap the mayor in the face to try to wake him up.

Mitch sees this as a good sign. If The Butcher is smacking the mayor in the face trying to wake him up, it must mean that there is still signs of life. He can see the eyes of the Mexican man as they seem to change from placid and calm to hyper and maniacal. In the proverbial blink of the eye, The Butcher has changed his entire body language. He now takes deliberate steps; his shoulders are no longer resting easy and his dark and rough skin is now glistening with sweat.

The intensity of the man has given Mitch new concerns. He can hear him saying things under his breath, he can't make out the words but the gravelly tone in the voice adds to the tension. El Carnicero climbs on top of the mayor's body quickly, like a vampire ready to attack his victim. His body straddles the chest as he raises a long blade high into the air. The knife had come from out of nowhere, obviously being hidden this whole time in his pocket. In a single swipe of his right arm, the blade slices through the neck of the mayor.

Blood flies high into the air from the arterial spray, covering The Butcher from head to waist. The irony of the man finally looking like a person in his namesake profession falls silently following the massacre. The killer sits softly on the chest of the mayor, taking a few long puffs from the cigar that has remained in his mouth for the entire length of the attack. He climbs down slowly, obviously unphased by the blood covering his face. He takes a moment to pull a handkerchief from his pocket to wipe his eyes before tossing it on the ground, where it falls quietly onto the rest of the pile of garbage.

As quickly as he had turned violent, The Butcher returns to the calmer demeanor with which he has carried himself all day. Methodically, he begins walking away from the now positively dead body of Harry Billings. He walks past the two fallen deputies without saying a word, choosing to blow more smoke into the air instead. Like fish out of water, the two squirm about trying to return to their original position, where they can see both The Butcher and the door where the trail of diesel fuel ends.

The cigar has nearly reached the end of its life in the man's mouth. Less smoke bellows with each breathe from the Mexican. The loose tobacco at the end blazes orange embers, daring to fall to the ground and set the entire building ablaze. The man uses his foot to hold the door open while he looks back a final time at Mitch and Sloane. He pulls the cigar from his mouth finally, looks at it as if it will speak to him, before turning his gaze on the officers.

"I was hoping your mayor would scream like a little coward. I guess I will just have to take my satisfaction from listening to you two burn." He repositions his foot to make sure that he can reach the floor to ignite the fuel while managing to keep the door open for an easy escape. "I thought you two would have put up more of a fight. I guess you are just like the rest of the Americans I have met, cowardly."

"You're awfully brave when I'm tied to a chair," Mitch contests.

"Do you really think if you weren't, you would be able to stop me?" As he finishes the sentence, he begins to lower the burning butt of the cigar to the concrete floor.

With the door propped open, the sheriff can see the streak coming toward the building. It took him a moment to realize what was happening, but once he did, he knew he had to distract The Butcher. "I don't know if I could have changed things, but I bet Deputy Johnson could."

Chapter 40

The realization as to what The Butcher was planning to do hit Deputy Johnson so quickly that he didn't have time to think. When he saw the Mexican crime boss standing in the doorway facing inside the warehouse, paired with the words shouted from Juan before he was gunned down, Stuart acted instinctively. He reached for the first thing he saw, the fire extinguisher that had been removed from the cab of the truck, and went running toward the door. He had forgotten about trying to move stealthily through the gravel, worrying more about stopping the man from lighting the building on fire.

As he gets closer, El Carnicero takes the cigar from his mouth and looks at it briefly. Stuart prays repeatedly that the man doesn't turn around and see him coming, but the man is focused on something inside the room. Stuart can hear words being said back and forth, but he is moving too quickly to process what is being said. Just before he reaches the doorway, The Butcher turns around unexpectedly. Their eyes meet for an instance, and Stuart thinks he can see a moment of fear in the Mexican's reaction.

With his forward momentum working in his favor, Stuart swings the fire extinguisher towards the head of The Butcher. The thud of the metal contacting the forehead echoes throughout the warehouse. The Mexican crumbles to the ground, his eyes rolling back in his head. Stuart's momentum forces him into the room where he too falls to the floor, never taking his eyes off the Mexican murderer. He sees the butt of the smoldering cigar roll through his fingers and onto the concrete floor.

It takes everything he has to respond quickly to the new threat. Stuart frantically tries to pull the pin from the extinguisher and after what seems like an eternity, he manages to figure it out. A long stream of white foam bellows from the extinguisher, covering the area where the cigar met the concrete, ending any threat of the fuel being ignited. If he had been a second later, the fuel would have engulfed the entire room, including Sheriff Thompson and Deputy Nichols. With the threat of fire nullified, Stuart drops the extinguisher at his feet and rushes over to his colleagues.

"Stuart, damn glad to see you. Get me out of here, it's not over." Mitch knows that the Arroyo brothers left carrying explosives with the idea of blowing up the entire town. "The Arroyo brothers have bombs and they're going to blow up the town. We got to find them."

"Well hello Sheriff. It's good to see you too," Stuart replies.

Mitch begins to get frustrated at the lack of urgency from Stuart. "I'm not kidding. We have to get out of here and find them, and we have to do it now!"

"Relax Mitch. We've already got the Arroyo boys."

The look of confusion on Mitch's face is obvious. "We? Who is we?" As he says this, he notices the man walking in from the same door where The Butcher was standing earlier.

"I think you know our friend Jesse Meyers," Stuart tells Mitch.

As the former soldier walks closer, he stops long enough to check the pulse of El Carnicero before joining the trio of officers in the middle of the room. Mitch looks up at Stuart. "I don't know what you're talking about Stuart. That's not Jesse Meyers, it's Ethan Ward."

"Well, whatever his name is, he was able to take care of the Arroyo brothers outside. I'm afraid he had to kill Juan." Stuart looks like he has had the weight of the world lifted from his shoulders in the last few minutes.

"He's not dead, I only shot him in the leg," Ethan chimes in.

"All I saw was him going down, I guess I just assumed. That will make it easier to explain when the Feds get here." Stuart says this as he takes a seat against the wall of the warehouse, thankful to have the ordeal behind him.

Once Mitch and Sloane have been untied and helped to their feet, The Feds start to arrive. Men can be seen inside and outside of the building, with one man stopping to give medical attention to the two officers. Mitch has several bumps and bruises, not to mention the multiple slashes made to his abdomen. Ethan tries to convince Mitch that he needs to go to the hospital in Portland, but Mitch pushes him away. He forces his way through the men and makes his way to Sloane. The two lovers look at each other for a moment before collapsing in a long hug.

There are no words exchanged between the two, but they both know how lucky they are to be able to walk away from this night. They had both considered the possibility of death, while Sloane had to contemplate the effects and consequences of far more heinous acts than Mitch did. They have been in this together and they both know that living through the experience will make them both stronger. It will make their relationship stronger.

"Mitch, I don't want to bother you, but is that Mayor Billings over there?" Stuart motions his hand toward the work bench where the body of Harry Billings lays covered in blood.

Mitch doesn't respond verbally, he just looks at Stuart and nods his head. This is the only communication that needs to be relayed. Stuart refrains from going over to investigate. Two of the federal agents have managed to handcuff The Butcher, who is now awake and leaning defeated against the wall near the door. Ethan makes his way to the Sheriff and shakes his hand.

"It's good to meet you Sheriff Thompson. My name is Ethan Ward." The two men look at each other as if they are friends keeping a secret, a look that is slightly more obvious than they are both aware.

"Thank you for all you did. You saved my life... again."

Sloane has been silent the whole time while the federal agents ask them questions and try to recount the events of the last couple of days. She has hung on tight to Mitch's waist, not wanting to let go. A thought enters her mind, something she hasn't thought about since she walked back onto the gravel lot of the trucking company.

"I hate to interrupt this collection of great male minds, but does anyone know what happened to the people that were in the trailer?" The faces of these people run through her mind and will probably haunt her for a long time.

"I saw them earlier this morning when I was coming out here, but not since," Stuart says.

"If they were illegals, chances are you'll never see them again," Ethan adds. "These people are survivors. We can't even begin to fathom the amount of shit they went through to get here. I don't think we need to worry about them. Right now, I'm more worried about Sheriff Thompson."

"I'm fine," Mitch insists.

"Honey, you've been through a lot. It's probably best to get you checked out."

"What time is it?" Mitch asks.

"A little after midnight," Stuart answers.

Mitch looks down at the gashes on his stomach before replying. "Take me over to Dr. Mike's house. He can stitch me up. Tomorrow is the parade and I need to be there."

"Mitch, Dr. Mike is retired! What is he going to do?" Stuart looks at the sheriff as if he is crazy.

"All I need is a couple of stitches. Dr. Mike is more than capable. There is no way I am going to miss the parade."

There are a few moments of silence before Sloane speaks up. "I'll take you over there, but I'm driving."

"Good to see you're back to normal," Mitch chuckles.

Sunday

Chapter 41

The car is silent as Mitch and Sloane make their way through town. It's nearly three in the morning and the streets of town are empty. There are chairs lining the curb of Main Street as visitors have marked their territory for the annual Labor Day parade. This time of year has always marked the end of the season and most residents hated to see the tourists go, along with their money. This year, Mitch is more than relieved that the craziness of the summer is coming to an end. Their town has been far too active for his liking, not to mention the loss of life that has accompanied the activity.

With the loss of adrenaline, the pain in his body has intensified. The spots on his stomach where the Arroyo brothers sliced through his skin are burning. He is struggling to find a position to sit in that doesn't aggravated his wounds more. Sloane insisted on driving and Mitch knows this was her attempt to reassert herself as an independent woman after looking so weak in the last few hours. He wants to say something to her, about how strong she really was, but he can't find the right words. He wants her to know that they would never have been able to survive had it not been for her. He wants to remind her of the lives of the strangers in the trailer who would be dead if not for her. He wants to tell her all these things, but he doesn't know where to start.

Sloane slides the car in front of Dr. Mike's house. Mitch has rarely visited the doctor since his childhood, but the man has lived in the same house for as long as the sheriff can remember. Sloane rushes to the passenger side of the car to help Mitch get out and the two officers struggle to climb the steps to the front porch. The doctor opens the door before they can even knock. Stuart, who remained at the trucking company to finish up with the F.B.I., called to let the doctor know they were coming. The grayed hair man opens the door wide and helps Mitch into the front room, throwing the sheriff's arm over his shoulder, allowing Mitch to rely on the big man for support.

Dr. Mike Joseph had been the only doctor in town for over thirty years. His job was a crucial one for the residents, who now must make the trip to a larger town whenever the need for serious medical procedures come up. Dr. Mike is a large man, not as much in height but in girth. Every time Mitch sees the man, he always has a smile on his face. Even now, after being woken from a sleep at this early hour, Dr. Mike still greets them with the face of a man who is more than willing to help.

Sloane waits in the front room as Mitch and Dr. Mike head to the back area, which Dr. Mike still refers to as his feel-good clinic. This gives the female officer a chance to look back on the events of the last few days. She was certain that things would turn out worse than they did. She is also relieved that the Mexicans decided to not sexually assault her. She was fearful of this, almost more worried about being sexually assaulted than she was about being killed. Her mind drifts to the faces of the people who she saved from the trailer. They looked so lost. They looked so desperate. She searches the corner of her mind, trying to remember every face as they jumped down and started walking away. This recollection has a soothing effect on her, and she quickly finds herself drifting asleep on the soft couch in the front room.

Sloane is startled awake by a knock at the front door. She had gotten so comfortable than when her eyes open, she has no idea where she is. After a few moments, she hears the doctor asking her to check the door to see who's there. Sloane opens the door and is attacked by Stuart as he pushes his way through the door and grabs her in a large bear hug. The sun has begun to rise, blinding Sloane as she looks over the older deputy's shoulder.

"Good morning Stuart. Did you bring me some coffee?" She pries her body out from the arms of the older man.

"I wish. The coffee shops don't open until later."

"You do know that you can make your own coffee, don't you?"

Stuart looks at her with a puzzled look, "I know that, but it tastes so much better when someone else makes it. How's the sheriff?"

Sloane turns and looks at the door that leads to the back room, slightly embarrassed that she had fallen asleep and has no idea how Mitch is doing. "I don't know Stuart, let's go check on him together."

Chapter 42

Dr. Mike welcomes the two officers into the room where Mitch is spread out on the floor. The only bed in the room is unusable, almost every corner of the room is now filled with boxes of paperwork, stacked two or three high. Since he has been retired for over five years, Dr. Mike has started taking down many of the things that decorated his office. The bed is now the final resting place for the educational tools, the torso that shows the muscles of the body and a life-sized skeleton. There are several white bandages on Mitch's chest and stomach, each one with a small circle of crimson blood showing through. The sheriff is sleeping when they enter the room but opens his eyes at the sound of the door closing.

"Hey Sheriff. I see you're awake," Stuart says with far too much energy.

"Hey. Yeah I'm awake." Mitch tries to sit up, but the soreness of his body doesn't allow it at first. Dr. Mike races over and slowly helps Mitch and props him against the nearby wall.

"I'm so glad you guys are alright. Most importantly, I'm glad I didn't die." The tall man slides down the wall so that he is sitting side by side with the sheriff, Sloane sits on the ground on the opposite side.

"Things got a little out of hand, that's for sure. There are still a few things I don't understand, blanks in the story. Now that we are all three together, maybe we can put the pieces together." Mitch looks up at Dr. Mike who takes the cue and exits the room without a word.

"I've told you just about everything from my end," Sloane says. "I drove the truck from the lot, noticed the blinking lights and tried to drop the trailer. Somehow, I ended up driving the truck down the side of the hill. When I woke up the next morning, I went looking for you and that's when Juan Arroyo grabbed me. After that we were together."

Stuart takes over after this, "I tried to get ahold of both of you when I got back from Portland with Mr. Billings."

'How is he?" Mitch interrupts.

"When I left, he was still alive. He'll never see again, but the doctors up there assured me it could have been far worse." Stuart pauses for a second before continuing to replay the events of the weekend from his perspective. "The next morning, I tried to get ahold of you two again and still had no luck. Both of your cars were still parked at your apartment complex."

Again, Mitch interrupts, "my truck broke down Thursday."

"Well that explains that. I'll get someone to look at your truck."

"Thanks Stuart. How did you get Ethan Ward involved?" All three of the officers know the real identity of the former soldier who saved them from the warehouse, but Mitch thinks the man has done enough to earn a pardon in their eyes.

"Well, the last thing I remember you saying you were going to do was talk to Mayor Billings. I drove to his place. I passed the herd of foreigners not long after I left town. When I parked behind your squad car, I started surveillance on the parking lot. That's when I saw Juan Arroyo grab Sloane." He stops here and looks over at her. "I mean Deputy Nichols. I knew there was nothing I could do alone, so I left and went looking for help. Ethan met me here later in the evening. I watched as he single-handedly captured the Arroyo brothers outside in the lot and then," Stuart stops abruptly, not wanting to relive what happened next.

"Then you came in and saved the day," Mitch says triumphantly. "Have the feds finished up their investigation?"

"Yeah they were finishing up when I left. Ethan had one of his men diffuse the bombs, don't ask me how. It's amazing what they teach soldiers these days."

"I guess we all owe our lives to Ethan," Sloane adds. "Without him, we probably didn't stand a chance."

The three officers let those words sink in for a moment, reflecting on how close they all were to becoming the latest victim of El Carnicero and his men. The trio of officers are relieved when Dr. Mike enters the room and breaks the tension.

"Doc, I sure do appreciate what you've done for me, but I need to get up. The parade starts in a few hours and we have to be there for crowd control."

"You're not going anywhere right now Mitch. I'm afraid the parade will have to go on without you this year," the doctor replies.

"It's alright Mitch. Ethan told me to tell you that he and his men will handle the parade. After what they did last night, I'm sure they are more than capable."

"I'll stay here with you Mitch," Sloane insists. "Let Ethan and his men handle it."

Mitch nods in defeat. Stuart rises to his feet and whispers something to Dr. Mike before looking back down at the Sheriff.

"I have to leave now but I'll be back before the parade, I've got some errands to run, mainly I need some coffee." This brings a smile to the sheriff's face. "I also want to get someone to look at your truck. Dr. Mike agreed to let me take you to the parade if we put you in the bed."

"Sure, I get sliced a few times in the chest and now you want to toss me in the back of the truck like a bag of garbage."

"Mitch, it will probably be the least painful way to get you around with your injuries," Sloane says.

"Look at the bright side Sheriff, this way you'll be sure to get a good seat for the parade. We can park in a handicapped space."

Kevin M. Moehring

Chapter 43

The room falls silent again after Stuart Johnson leaves. Sloane rests her head on Mitch's shoulder and the two are content to just sit next to each other. This is the first chance that Mitch has had to reflect on the atrocities of the night. As he closes his eyes briefly, he is hit with the lasting image of The Butcher slicing the throat of Mayor Billings. The amount of blood that escaped was unbelievable. His mind then flashed to the image of the Mexican man walking past him, covered in blood and puffing on his cigar. Mitch smiles as his recollection turns to Stuart swinging the fire extinguisher like a baseball bat and the unforgettable sound of the metal striking flesh and bone.

"What happens now?" Sloane asks the question as if she's speaking out of turn. Rarely is her voice this quiet and timid.

"I'm assuming the feds will take care of everything. They will be here soon to question us and get our statements. Since the Arroyo brothers and The Butcher are from Mexico, and I'm sure they are wanted by several federal agencies, we will have no say in the investigation or what happens to them."

"That's not what I meant. We have been through a lot in a short time. I meant, what happens to us next?"

Mitch hadn't really pondered the question before he heard it. Is she asking for him to propose or have the unfortunate events they've had to face together forced her to realize she may be safer to distance herself from him?

"I'm not sure what you're asking. Just like after Graham Park and everything else that happened this summer, things will go back to normal. You've never seen Twisted Timbers during the offseason."

"Mitch, I'm not worried about this case or being in town during the offseason. I'm asking what you are going to do from here. What are we going to do once all the smoke settles?"

"I guess we go back to life as normal. I love you and I want us to be able to go back to the way things were before these guys came to town."

Sloane doesn't respond right away, causing Mitch to fear that she no longer wants the same things as he does. When she does finally speak, the shyness in her tone is replaced with the firm and authoritative voice that he is used to hearing.

"Things are changing around here Mitch. Ms. Reynolds is going to build a big resort in town. Stuart is probably going to quit the department."

"Wait, why do you say that? Did he tell you that?"

"No Mitch, he didn't, but sometimes you have to open your eyes and look around. For the smartest man I know, sometimes you can be really naïve. The man is afraid to leave the office and do any actual police work. If I had seen him get captured by Juan Arroyo would, I have run away and looked for help?"

"Probably not," Mitch concedes. "But you would have been caught just like he would have been. Stuart has been a cop for a long time, and this is how things have been around here for a long time."

"Look, I love you, but you have to open your eyes. This thing is going to be all over the news, just like everything else that has happened this summer." Sloane has now gotten to her feet and is looking down on Mitch with imploring eyes. "I want to be here, and I

315

want to be with you, but things are changing all around and you are the only one refusing to acknowledge it."

"I still don't know what you want from me. I know things in this town are different from most other places. I also know that what has happened here is not the norm. Things like this can't keep happening, it's impossible." He tries to sit up straighter so he can look her in the eyes, grunting with every movement of his body.

"Do you need me to spell it out for you. I need security in my life. I need to know that no matter what happens, to me or to this town, that you will be there for me. I need to longer hide the fact that I love you. If we are going to live together, I want the world to know it. I don't want to be one of those women who mourn for the love of their life in private."

The conversation has turned in a direction Mitch hadn't expected. What had begun as a rant about how Mitch needed to change who he was and how he did things, has now turned into her asking if he is going to protect her and always be with her. He extends his arm to her, inviting her to come back and lay on him. Sloane looks down, resisting the urge as long as she can before rejoining him on the ground.

"Look Sloane, I know who you are and what you need. You know who I am and what I am about. I want to be with you. I need to be with you. If you're looking for a commitment from me, you got it."

"I don't want you to just say things because I bring them up. I need to know that no matter what happens in this town, I am still your number one priority. You are all I have left."

Mitch has tried to force out the images of most of the things that happened in the warehouse overnight. Her words bring these memories back in full color. "You have no idea how I felt when I thought you were dead. I gave up. I stopped fighting. I didn't want to go on knowing that I was unable to protect you."

She snuggles in a little closer, squeezing a little too tight to his ribs and causing him to moan. "Then I guess you need to get a little better at protecting me in the future, because I'm not going anywhere."

Kevin M. Moehring

Chapter 44

They had remained snuggled together, asleep on the floor for a couple of hours and would have remained there longer if they had not heard the words coming from the other room. The door to the room they're in is opened as Dr. Mike ushers in a few guys in cheap suits. Much like Mitch had anticipated, the F.B.I. has shown up to ask them questions. Seeing these federal officers has become too frequent for Mitch's liking over the last few months, although many of the faces he sees now are new to him.

The agents ask questions over and over, writing diligently in their notebooks as Mitch and Sloane answer as best they can, each of them adding to the story in the parts when they were separated. The agents also try to fill in the gaps when needed. Mitch had no idea at the realm of activity that had been going on in town throughout the summer. The lead agent tells him that The Butcher has been on their most wanted list for several years.

The amount of drugs, weapons and illegal immigrants that had come through the small town is staggering. The F.B.I. had been investigating the increase of activity on the west coast, but they had hit a brick wall once the ships from Mexico hit the ports in the U.S. They explain that the most logical path would be for the mayor's trucks to meet the cargo at the port, transport it back it the trucking yard where the contraband would be divided and distributed throughout the country.

Sloane asks the man about the people she freed from the trailer on Saturday morning. The agent tells her a similar story as to what Ethan Ward relayed to her earlier. The people risked everything they had to make the journey to this country. Once they are here, they are set free and forced to fend for themselves or else used as human slaves for the people who brought them here. Starting from scratch in a country like this is far easier than having to do it in Mexico. Sloane listens intently but can't stop the tears from forming in her eyes.

The meeting continues for several more minutes and is only interrupted when Dr. Mike enters the room and hands Mitch a telephone. The agents leave the room, giving the sheriff his privacy. Sloane leans in close to Mitch trying to hear as much as she can from whomever is on the other end of the line.

"Hello?" Mitch answers hesitantly. He remains silent for some time and even when he does speak, he only does so in the positive. "Yes sir," followed by more silence, then a "I think that's the smart thing." Mitch turns and looks at Sloane who has given up trying to hear what the conversation is about. "I will let him know sir. Thanks for calling."

Mitch hands the phone back to Dr. Mike, who takes it and leaves the room once again. Sloane sits patiently and twiddles her thumbs in a playful nature. She wants to know what the conversation was about, but she doesn't want to ask. She knows Mitch well enough to know when he is messing with her, and this is one of those times. Luckily for him, the tension is eased when Stuart returns to the room.

"Good to see you two are looking better. Sloane, I brought you some coffee." He hands here the pale brown liquid in the colorful green cup before taking a sip of his own beverage.

"Thanks Stuart but this looks more like sewer water than coffee." She takes the drink from him and sits it on the table without drinking from it.

"I got good news. I had Elmer down at the garage look at your truck this morning. Turns out the old thing just needed a new serpentine belt and a couple of filters. It's good to go."

"Thanks Stuart. Did the Feds talk to you here?"

"I saw them boys over at the trucking yard and gave them my story. They were all leaving as I was coming in." The tall deputy nervously drinks more of his fancy coffee from the straw.

Mitch searches the room for a clock but doesn't see one. "Do we have time to make it to the parade?"

"We do but it may be close. I know the perfect parking place but we're only going to make it on time if we let Sloane drive." Stuart looks apologetically at the female officer. "No offense, but you kind of drive like a banshee. I'll sit in the back with the sheriff."

"No offense taken." Sloane stands up and makes sure her uniform is tucked in. "I've always wanted to park in a handicapped spot."

Chapter 45

The three officers give their regards to Dr. Mike and leave the house together, Mitch using the shoulders of the other two to hold his weight. His feet hit the ground softly, but the sutures in his chest bark at him with every step. It takes some creativity to get him in the back of the truck without hurting him further, including an ill-placed hand by Stuart Johnson. Once Mitch is slid all the way toward the cab, sitting up as comfortable as an injured man can, Stuart joins him in the back and Sloane fires up the old truck.

Mitch has never been in the back of a moving truck before and isn't sure if it's the road or the driver that makes him fear for his life. "Man, you were right, she does drive like a banshee," he says to Stuart, loud enough to be heard over the rusting exhaust.

Stuart simply smiles back in agreement. Since the truck left the driveway, the older deputy has been staring off in the distance. Mitch knows what's coming, the news given to him from Sloane during their discussion earlier.

"Mitch, we need to talk. I love my job. Well, I used to love my job. I just don't think I can do it anymore." He still has not looked over at Mitch. "I am not cut out for the dangerous side of the job. I almost crapped my pants when I saw Juan Arroyo yesterday."

"Stuart, I understand. Do you want to be on desk duty? I'm not sure how much longer Lucille will keep working." Mitch leans his body closer to his deputy while still maintaining a tight grip on the side of the truck as it jostles him around.

"I think I just want to resign. I don't know what I am going to do after this, but I know I am not made out to be a police officer." He finally turns to look at Sheriff Thompson and a single tear escapes his eye.

"You've been a cop as long as I can remember. It won't be the same without you."

The two men share a look and turn their attention to the buildings along Main Street and the collection of people that are crowded along the curb. Mitch wonders how long he can let this charade play out. He knew Stuart was going to resign and even if he didn't, even if he found some inner strength to continue with the department, Mitch knew that Stuart was destined for greater things.

Sloane pulls the truck into the lone handicapped spot in town, right outside the police station and city hall. From this vantage point they will be able to see every float that comes down the street and they will easily be able to hear the high school marching band. Before Sloane comes around to join them, Mitch lets Stuart know about the call he got at Dr. Mike's house. The older deputy hops down from the bed of the truck and races into city hall after hearing the details.

Sloane makes her way to the back of the truck and slides into Mitch's arms. They sit silently and watch as the parade starts up, ecstatic to have the town celebrating together even though nobody knows how close the town had come to being destroyed. The band marches by, playing the familiar school fight song.

Once the music passes, Sloane takes the opportunity to question Mitch further. "Where did Stuart race off to?"

"I don't know. I guess he had to use the bathroom or something. You know how much coffee that man drinks," Mitch replies, not yet ready to reveal his secret.

"And what about that call you got at the Doc's house?"

"What about it?"

"Are you going to tell me what it was about?" Sloane knows he is playing with her and her cheeks begin to turn a darker shade of pink.

"You want to know?"

"Yes, I do," she says.

"I mean, do you really want to know?" Mitch is loving every second of the playful banter.

"If you don't tell me, I'll make sure you sleep in the back of this truck tonight," she says.

Mitch holds his hands up in mock surrender and points back to the parade. The final entrant every year is reserved for the mayor of the town. Nobody had really considered the implications of the death of Mayor Billings as it pertained to the parade, most of the town still didn't know the man was dead. The city council, however, knows how important it is for the visitors to see business as usual. They wanted someone to ride in the parade as the mayor, a face to show the guests that they are welcome to return the following season. The members of the city council acted quickly to come up with a suitable replacement for Mayor Billings and quickly realized Stuart was the most qualified. Since there are no elections in town for local matters, it was quickly voted on by council and Stuart was offered the position.

Judging by the smile Stuart is now shining while waving from the back of the bright red convertible, he accepted the offer. Mitch looks at the man in all his glory. He thinks for a brief second about how his father would have loved to have Stuart Johnson as the mayor of town.

"Stuart is the new mayor?" Sloane breaks in to interrupt Mitch's thoughts.

"The title fits him don't you think?"

"Is this what the phone call was about?"

"The council called to ask my thoughts and they wanted me to be the one to tell him. I decided to have a little fun with Stuart and not tell him what was up until we got here. By the way, you were right."

"Right about what?"

"He tried to tell me he was quitting on the way here."

"Somebody jot this down," Sloane screams. "On this date, Mitch Thompson actually agreed that I was right."

"If you keep it up, you'll be sleeping in the truck!"

Sloane smirks. "Well this turned out to be a pretty good day."

Mitch pulls her closer, "You're right. The town's safe, my truck is fixed, and I got my best girl sitting next to me. Life don't get much better."

She gives him a slight elbow on the arm, "Well if that wasn't the cheesiest thing you ever said. If I didn't know any better, I'd think you were reading the lines of an old country song."

Mitch's laugh cuts through the sounds from the mass of cheering onlookers. "Well then if that's the case, just remember, I'm going to love you, forever and ever, forever and ever, Amen."

Kevin M. Moehring

I hope you have enjoyed Town on Fire. Please remember that reviews are the best way to let other readers know how you felt about the book.

To stay up to date with upcoming projects and book signing appearances from the author, follow him on Facebook and Twitter.

Kevin M. Moehring